Assault on England

I had stupidly allowed myself to be captured and stuffed into the back seat of the sedan. I cursed audibly as the car carried me toward a watery grave in the Thames. I had to escape. A thug on my left was gazing out of the window, but his buddy had a .45 revolver pointed at my head. So I had to divert his attention.

'Watch out!' I yelled suddenly. My guards looked forward instinctively. I slammed down hard on the gun arm of the man on my right and finished him off with a chop to the throat. As the other agent grabbed my arm, I rammed an elbow into his face, breaking his nose. Then I shoved the driver headlong into the windshield and leaped out of the side door just as the car crashed into a utility pole. I ran to the main road.

There was work to do.

Assault on England

Nick Carter

TANDEM
14 Gloucester Road, London, SW7

Originally published in the United States by
Universal Publishing & Distributing Corporation, 1972

Published in Great Britain by Universal-Tandem
Publishing Co. Ltd, 1973

Made and printed in Great Britain by
Hunt Barnard Printing Ltd., Aylesbury, Bucks.

Dedicated to
The Men of the Secret Services
of the
United States of America

Prologue

It was one of those days for Henry Wellsey, Britain's 55-year-old Chancellor of the Exchequer. It started at breakfast when his wife brought up the subject of a holiday again.

'You must have a proper holiday, you haven't had one in over a year. Weekends at Bayberry Hall simply don't count . . . '

Bayberry Hall, his mother's estate in Yorkshire, didn't count for much with Milicent anyway, he knew.

'You want someplace warm and relaxing. Spain, perhaps, or Italy. Or Yugoslavia . . . they say the Dalmatian Coast is marvelous.'

'They'd probably say I was defecting,' Wellsey said dryly, sipping his cocoa.

'Don't be absurd,' his wife snapped. 'Now don't try and put me off, Henry. You must see about a holiday. I warn you, if you don't, I'll speak to the Prime Minister myself!'

She would too, Wellsey thought glumly, sitting in the back of his Rolls 30 minutes later, and the P.M. was not in a holiday mood. It wasn't going to improve either. There was a special cabinet meeting that morning at the Prime Minister's residence and Wellsey was going to be late. A gray Jaguar and a lorry, arguing – fatally – over the right of way, had the London-bound traffic all tied up. It was liable to be another hour before the police cleared the accident scene.

Wellsey didn't miss all of the cabinet meeting; it dragged on through lunch. The Chancellor left Number 10 Downing Street feeling frustrated, as he so often did lately. International issues always seemed to take precedence over domestic ones. On impulse, he stopped at Cook's for some travel brochures. Maybe Milicent was right; maybe it *was* time for a holiday.

Back at his office, he'd just settled down at his desk when his secretary came in with the mail.

'Could you bring me some tea, Miss Tanner? I know it's a bit early but . . . '

'Certainly, sir.' Miss Tanner, not too young, not too pretty but efficient, smiled.

Wellsey picked up the top letter and a letter opener – he liked to open his mail himself – but he put them down again and took out the brochures he'd collected at Cook's instead. He leaned back in his chair, studying them. Spain . . . the Costa Brava . . . Very nice, he understood, and not crowded at this time of year, the man at Cook's had said. Italy . . . Rome . . . Venice . . . sinking into the sea supposedly. He shook his head. 'Tour the Greek Islands.' Now, that was a thought. He'd been to Athens but never to the islands. Mykonos . . . Lelos . . . Rhodes . . . Lovely . . .

The last thing Henry Wellsey saw in this world was the smiling face of a pretty young Greek girl holding an armful of red, red roses. The high-powered 7mm rifle bullet that entered the back of his head at the base of the skull made a fairly neat entry hole, considering it had to pass through the closed window first, but it smashed on through bone and tissue and when it exited, Wellsey's face disintegrated.

He slumped forward, his blood blending with the red of the roses of Rhodes.

Miss Tanner came in with the tea and found him and could not stop screaming . . .

One

The night was sticky-hot and airless on the Luxor docks. On one side loomed the wharf buildings, squatting heavily in the blackness. On the other, the Nile slipped soundlessly by on its journey to Cairo and the sea. Beyond the river stretched the desert, a lighter strip between the oily black water and the star-pocked sky.

Waiting on that desolate black waterfront I touched Wilhelmina, the 9mm Luger I carry in a special shoulder holster, to reassure myself. A crawly feeling at the back of my neck warned me I might need her tonight.

I was there on Hawk's orders to contact a small-time smuggler and gambler named Augie Fergus. Fergus had sent a wire from Luxor to the Prime Minister of England saying he had information for sale that might shed light on the brutal assassination of Britain's Chancellor of the Exchequer, Henry Wellsey. Since the British didn't have an agent in the area at the moment, Hawk had volunteered my services.

Fergus had told me on the phone that he would meet me on the docks at midnight. I glanced at my watch; it was already fifteen minutes past. That alone was enough to make me wary, and I was thinking about leaving when I heard a sound in the darkness.

I glanced quickly at a small door leading into the warehouse behind me. It had opened and now a man came out. He was of medium height and growing bald. He wore a gray suit that looked like it had been slept in for a week. But the thing about him that I noticed immediately was his eyes. They were opened wide, bloodshot, and darted furtively left and right, missing nothing. I'd seen those eyes before, on hundreds of men. They were the eyes of someone frightened out of his wits, of someone a step ahead of death.

'Carter?' he whispered, afraid that the night would hear him.

I nodded.

He swung the door wider and motioned me inside. As I entered he pulled a string and the room was flooded with light from a naked bulb that hung from the ceiling. It was a small room, and the only furniture in it was a cracked, stained washstand in the corner and a soiled mattress on the floor. Strewn about were crumpled newspapers and empty brown bags. The heady aroma of garlic and onions permeated the air.

Augie Fergus withdrew a pint bottle of liquor from his jacket pocket and with trembling hands managed to uncap it and drink long and hard. When he finished, he had calmed down somewhat.

'The information, Fergus,' I said impatiently. 'What is it?'

'Not so fast,' he countered. 'Not until I get 5,000 pounds and a private flight to Khartoum. When I get there safely, you'll get your bloody information.'

I thought about it, but not for long. Five thousand pounds is a damn cheap price to pay for what he had to offer. I could have London wire the British consulate in Luxor instructing them to give me the money. And hiring a private plane wouldn't be too hard. I agreed to his terms, but warned him what would happen to him if he tried anything funny.

'It's on the up-and-up, mate,' he whined.

'Okay,' I said. 'I'll have the money tomorrow afternoon. I'll fly you out then.'

Fergus shook his head. 'Tomorrow night, this time. 'Ell, the whole bloody city's crawling with bastards after me. In broad daylight I'll be spotted.'

'Who's after you, Fergus, and why?'

'None of your business,' he shot back. 'It's got nothing to do with the killing in London. It's personal. Just be here tomorrow night with the money and a way out of here.'

'If that's the way you want it . . .' I shrugged and turned to leave.

'Carter,' Fergus called out as I reached the door, 'one more thing. If anything should happen to me, go to the Grand Hotel bar in Tangiers. Someone will contact you there with the information.'

'How will I know him?'

'Don't worry,' he said, 'my person will know you. Just hand over the money and you'll get what you want.'

I nodded and left.

I had to wait until morning for the telegraph office to open. When it did, I wired London for the money. Three hours later I got my reply. The consulate had been instructed to release 5,000 pounds to me. After collecting the money I reserved a charter plane at the airport. There were still eight hours left before my meeting with Fergus. I returned to my room, showered, ordered a gin and tonic. Then I went to sleep.

I was awakened by my alarm clock at eight in the evening. I dressed, gathered up the attache case of money and took a cab to Fergus' hideout.

This time the door was opened by a stranger. He was a short, rather thin Arab wearing a white tropical suit and a red fez.

He said nothing to me but grinned and motioned toward the open door with his left hand; his right, I noted, was stuck in his jacket pocket.

Another man came out, a large heavy Arab wearing

14

the traditional desert garb of kaffiyeh, robe and sandals.

'Mr Carter?' he said. 'Mr Nick Carter?'

I had not used a cover name with Augie; there had seemed little point. 'That's right,' I said.

'You have come to meet Augie Fergus.'

He wasn't asking, he was telling. I squinted, trying to see better in the darkness. 'Right again,' I said, watching the thin man with his hand in his pocket. 'Where is he?'

The fat man smiled. 'He is here, Mr Carter. You will see him. In the meantime, let us introduce ourselves. I am Omar ben Ayoub.' He watched me closely, obviously expecting some reaction. 'And this is my associate, Gasim.'

'If Fergus is here,' I said, ignoring the introductions, 'where is he?'

Ayoub, in turn, ignored my question. 'You would assist Augie Fergus in cheating his colleagues, would you, Mr Carter? You would help him leave Luxor without paying his debts.'

'I don't know what the hell you're talking about,' I snapped at him. 'But I want to see Augie and I want to see him now.'

Ayoub's smile disappeared. 'All right, Mr Carter,' he said grimly. 'You shall see him.'

He snapped his fingers and two more Arabs appeared in the black doorway, big husky men in western suits. They were dragging something, the limp body of a man. They dragged it to within a few feet of me and dropped it unceremoniously on the dock.

'Augie Fergus,' Ayoub said, satisfaction in his smooth voice.

I looked down at the corpse at my feet, my face expressionless, my stomach tight. It was Fergus, all right. He had been killed with a knife, or some other sharp instrument, and it had happened slowly. The body was badly mutilated.

'Augie found out what happens to those who do not deal scrupulously with Omar ben Ayoub. And now, Mr Carter, you will find out.' Ayoub nodded at the two big men who had dumped Fergus at my feet and suddenly they had knives in their hands, the long wicked-looking kind the Bedouins of the desert carry. I thought of Hugo, the pencil-thin stiletto strapped to my right forearm. But Hugo couldn't do me much good at the moment. Besides the two muscle boys, Ayoub's skinny buddy, Gasim, had that lump in his jacket pocket pointed at me.

The two knife men moved in. One of them was a bit heavier than the other and slower moving, but he came in first. I figured they weren't out to kill me with the first cut. They wanted me to die slowly, like Augie.

Number One came in, swinging the knife at my belly. I jerked back a step and the knife razored through my jacket. I had no time to go for Wilhelmina. The big man swiped at me, again putting his weight behind it. I stepped to one side and punched a short jab into his neck as he went by.

He grunted and whirled back toward me angrily.

The second knife man had hovered just a few feet away. Now, with a sudden burst of speed, he came in on my left. He swung his knife low, toward my rib cage. I turned toward him and caught the knife arm, turned the wrist downward and in, at the same time dropping to one knee and throwing the man over my shoulder. He went flying, hitting the dock hard at his buddy's feet, narrowly missing knocking him down.

The first bull dodged, then charged, holding his knife straight out in front of him. I heard Ayoub shout: 'Get him! Get him!' in Arabic, and then the bull was on me, the knife stabbing toward my abdomen. I brought the edge of my hand down hard on the outstretched knife-arm as I twisted away from the thrust and heard bone snap. The bull screamed and the knife clattered to the dock. As the man plummeted past me, I chopped at his thick neck and felt vertebrae crunch under the impact. He slammed face down on the dock.

'Kill him! Kill him!' Ayoub was screaming now. Out of the corner of my eye, I saw that Gasim had pulled the gun out of his jacket and was aiming it at me.

The slug missed my head by inches and almost hit the second knife man as he came in. I grabbed his knife arm, twisted, and we went down together.

We hit the dock next to the corpse of Augie Fergus. We rolled onto and over the body, wrestling for the knife, Gasim dancing around us awkwardly, trying to get a shot off, but afraid to fire because he might hit the wrong man.

'Shoot! Shoot!' Ayoub shrieked at him.

I had to do something fast. The knifer was on top of me now. I squeezed my knee up, rammed it into his groin. He bellowed, fell to one side. I smashed a fist into his face as he fell. Gasim had stopped dancing now and was aiming carefully at my head.

I flexed my right forearm in a way I had practiced hundreds of times and Hugo slipped into my hand. The knife man was getting up and I hurled Hugo at him. The stiletto turned over once and buried itself in the Arab's throat. As Hugo left my hand I did a quick roll; Gasim's shot splintered wood where my head had been.

I rolled a second time as Gasim fired again. I came up, reaching for the Luger in my jacket.

My first shot missed Gasim's head by inches, but the second slammed into his chest, spinning him into the wall of the warehouse behind him. His gun went flying.

I turned and saw that Ayoub had decided to make a run for it. I didn't want to shoot; I wanted to find out what he knew about Augie Fergus, so I sprinted after him, dived for him headlong.

We went down, hitting the dock together. Unluckily we landed near an iron bar some workman had left on the dock. Ayoub grabbed at it desperately, swung it at me. He meant to crush my skull but the blow glanced off my neck and shoulder. It was enough, though, to

knock Wilhelmina out of my grasp and send rockets
of pain shooting up my arm.

Ayoub was back on his feet, still holding the iron
bar. Wilhelmina had landed somewhere near the edge
of the dock. I stumbled over there, spotted the Luger
and bent to retrieve it.

But Ayoub, moving surprisingly fast for a fat man,
charged me with the bar. He was going to end it once
and for all – I could see it in his eyes. I couldn't bring
Wilhelmina up in time, Ayoub was moving too fast.
As he swung the bar, I stepped aside and let him move
on past me. The next minute he was in mid-air
over the black water and then he splashed into the
Nile.

He came up sputtering. The current was taking him
and he thrashed around wildly. Obviously he couldn't
swim. His head went under but he came up again,
choking. The kaffiyehed head went under once more.
Only a few bubbles rose to the surface this time, then
the river was tranquil again.

I walked back up the dock to reclaim Hugo. Both
of the muscle boys were dead, but Gasim wasn't – I
heard him groan. I slipped Hugo back into his sheath
and, holding Wilhelmina loosely at my side, advanced
cautiously to where Gasim lay near the wall of the
warehouse.

When I saw the man's condition, I holstered the
Luger and squatted beside him. He stared up at me
with glazed eyes.

'What was Augie Fergus to you and Ayoub?' I

asked. 'If you don't want me to leave you to die, you'd better talk.' He was dead already but didn't know it.

He groaned, moving his head from side to side in pain. 'Fergus,' he gasped, 'smuggled . . . ancient treasures . . . out of country for us. He was overheard . . . say . . . intended leave without paying Ayoub . . . last consignment. Some . . . American was to fly him . . . Khartoum . . . private plane. Ayoub thought you . . . that man.'

He coughed and appeared about ready to give up. I propped his head up. 'And what about the information Fergus had for the British government?' I asked. 'Was Ayoub in on that?'

Gasim's glazed eyes searched for mine. 'British government?'

I saw no point in being coy about things now. 'Yes, the telegram Augie sent the Prime Minister. The information he had about the assassination of Henry Wellsey. Was Ayoub to profit from that?'

'I know nothing . . . of this,' Gasim gasped. 'Neither . . . did Ayoub.'

Suddenly he stiffened in my hands, then went limp. He was dead.

I lowered his head and knelt there for a moment in the blackness. By accident I had gotten mixed up in one of Augie Fergus's shady deals – had, ironically, almost gotten myself killed – and I still didn't know anything about the assassination. It was possible, of course, that Ayoub had known something without telling Gasim. But it didn't matter now one way or the other. Both Augie and Ayoub were beyond further explanation or conniving.

The next day I took a United Arab Airlines flight to Cairo and grabbed the next jet to Tangier. I arrived in Tangier and first took a room at the Grand Hotel, in the Medina, which Fergus had mentioned. I had lunch in a nearby restaurant, mechoui and a Stork Pils beers, then returned to the hotel bar.

I was sipping a Pernod, standing beside a barstool with my back to the dark-mustached bartender, when the girl came in. She was young, dressed in a black sheath and high-heeled sandals. Long straight dark hair fell over her shoulders. She was beautiful the way only young Arabian girls can be beautiful: a dark, earthy beauty with a hint of mystery. She walked in a way that made a man want to reach out and touch her, a hips-undulating, breasts-moving, sensual walk that made an erotic but not vulgar display of her body. I watched as she moved past me, avoiding my eyes, leaving a faint scent of musky perfume in the air. She sat on a barstool about halfway down the bar and ordered a sherry. After the bartender had served her, he moved down to me.

'Every day she comes in like this,' he said, noticing my admiring glance. 'She orders one drink – just the one – and then she leaves.'

'She's lovely,' I said. 'Do you know her name?'

'It is Hadiya – in Arabic it means "gift",' he said,

smiling through his mustache. 'She dances at the Miramar Hotel. Shall I introduce you?'

I picked up my Pernod. 'Thanks,' I said, 'but I'll go it solo.'

The girl turned to look at me as I sat down beside her. Her eyes, big and black, were even lovelier close up, but at the moment aloof and wary. 'May I buy you a drink?' I asked.

'Why?' she said coolly.

'Because you remind me of five memorable days I spent in Lebanon,' I said, 'and because it pleases me to be near you.'

She looked into my eyes and studied my face for a long moment. 'All right,' she said suddenly. 'You remind me of three lovely days in Gibraltar.'

We laughed then together, and her laugh was musical. We exchanged names and some small talk about Tangier, and then the bartender showed up.

'A call for you.'

I groaned inwardly. It was Hawk, I knew. His plane must have arrived early. I asked Hadiya to wait for me and excused myself. I took the call in the lobby, for privacy.

'Nick?' The voice was brisk, businesslike, with just a hint of a New England accent.

'Yes, sir. I hope you had a good flight.'

'The girls were pretty, but the food was terrible,' Hawk grated. I pictured his lean, impatient face, capped by thick graying hair, as he sweated in the Tangier airport telephone booth. 'I have only a few hours between flights, Nick, so kiss the girl goodbye, whoever she is, and meet me at the Djenina Restaurant for an early dinner in exactly ... one hour and a half.'

I acknowledged and the phone clicked in my ear. I stood there for a moment, wondering what Hawk had up his sleeve for me now and whether it would be a follow-up to the Luxor business. Then I returned to the girl. 'I have to leave,' I said. 'Business.'

'Oh,' she said, pouting prettily.

'But I think I'll catch the floor show at the Miramar tonight,' I said. 'If it's at all possible.'

'I would like that, Mr Carter.' She smiled at me.

I drew back. 'I told you my first name, not my last.'

'Augie Fergus told me you'd be here,' she said.

'How the hell did ... '

Her face grew solemn. 'Augie called me yesterday afternoon from Luxor. He described you, then said if anything happened to him, I should give you a photograph he keeps in his suitcase in our room.'

Somehow, the thought of this beautiful thing belonging to Augie Fergus took me by surprise, and I must have registered it. I opened my mouth to say something, but she cut me short.

'Something has gone wrong, then?' she asked.

I gave her the details. She took it all passively, then said, 'It must have happened while he was on the telephone.'

'What must have happened?' I asked.

23

'When he was killed. He was saying, "Tell Carter that . . ." when the line went dead.'

'That's all he managed to say?'

She shook her head up and down.

'Nothing more?'

'Nothing.'

'I've got the money here,' I patted the attache case at my side. 'Give me the photograph.'

'It's in my room,' she said. 'Meet me tonight, after the show. I'll give it to you then.'

'Now I know I'll catch the show,' I said.

'Do that,' she smiled, then slid off her barstool and walked out.

I walked to the Djenina Restaurant in the Casbah. Most of my meetings with Hawk were at his offices in the Amalgamated Press and Wire Services building on DuPont Circle in Washington. Rarely did we confer outside of Washington or New York, rarer still outside of the U.S. Hawk had no love for junkets about the globe and ventured abroad only on matters of the most extreme urgency. He apparently had classified his Johannesburg visit – and our Tangier meeting – as urgent.

Hawk arrived a short time after me and we took an outside table. He looked almost English, in a tweed jacket and gray trousers. His face was lined and looked tired and his spare frame seemed even slimmer than usual.

'Bad luck at Luxor, Nick. Damned bad luck. But maybe you'll get something from the girl.' He pulled a long brown cigar from his jacket, stuck it into his mouth and chewed down on it without lighting it. 'You probably haven't seen it in the papers yet but there's been another assassination in London.' He removed the cigar from his mouth and watched my reaction.

'Another government official?' I asked.

'You might say so. This time it's Percy Dumbarton, Britain's Minister of Defence.'

I whistled and stared out across the narrow cobble-stoned street, through the slow traffic of robed Arabs and donkey carts to the crumbling old buildings across the way. I started to comment, but just then the waiter returned to take our order. I ordered the Moroccan chicken couscous, and Hawk stuck to steak. Then the waiter was gone again.

'Dumbarton,' Hawk continued not waiting for my response, 'was one of England's most able leaders. The killer left another note, and it's clear now that the threat in the first note was no idle one.'

'You haven't filled me in on that,' I reminded him.

Hawk reached into his pocket again and handed me two pieces of paper. 'Here. I've typed out what the two notes said. Top one's the first one.'

I read: 'This is to prove we mean business. To prevent the death of other cabinet members, the British government must arrange to pay to us the sum of ten million pounds within the fortnight. Another execution will occur each fortnight until payment is made and the sum will increase by two million pounds after each succeeding death.

'The British government will save important lives, considerable anguish and millions of pounds sterling by immediate capitulation to our demand. When that inescapable decision is reached, a white flag must be flown below the Union Jack atop Parliament. At that signal, a further note will be delivered advising method of payment.'

I looked up at Hawk. 'Interesting,' I said. Then I read the second note, the original of which had been found at the scene of the second assassination:

'You were warned but you did not take us seriously. Now your Minister of Defence is dead, and our demand has risen to twelve million pounds. Is the government of Britain too proud to capitulate? Let us hope not. We will watch for the white flag.'

I shook my head slowly. 'What do the British make of it?' I asked.

'They don't know *what* to make of it, N3,' Hawk said grimly. 'They're literally running around in circles. These were particularly bloody murders and panic is growing in high places. There is talk that even the Queen isn't safe. It's the biggest thing in years. It could literally destroy the British government if they don't find out what it's all about.'

The waiter was back with the food. Hawk attacked the steak eagerly, talking as he ate.

'At first they thought it might be one of the international crime syndicates. Or maybe even an ex-con, recently released, with a grudge against official London. Now they think it may be the Russians.'

I was skeptical. 'Really?'

'It may not be as farfetched as it sounds. The Russians are at odds, bitterly, with several of Britain's top leaders. Dumbarton was one of them. They might be trying to effect a change of government in London – the direct way. It's been done before.'

Hawk finished his steak and leaned back. 'Maybe Russia is more edgy than we think,' he continued. 'Dumbarton was pushing the development of a fighter aircraft that would make a MIG look like Von Richtofen's Fokker DR-1. He was also pressing for a bacterial arsenal. British intelligence points to the language of the notes – the repetitive use of "we" and "us," the fact that the note paper is the same kind used by a Russian sub-agent in another matter. And, lastly, to the fact that Boris Novosty, who recently showed up in London, has now mysteriously dropped out of sight.'

'He's one of KGB's best,' I said thoughtfully.

Hawk nodded.

'And that's why you're here. The chief of SOE's Select Missions group and the Prime Minister got together and decided that since you're already in on this thing through Augie Fergus, and especially because Novosty and his people have never seen you, it would be nice if I loaned you to them for a while.'

'And thus ends another brief but glorious holiday,'

I said. 'I just wish I had been able to get something from Fergus.'

'He may not have had anything,' Hawk said. 'The most they could find out about the poor devil is that he served as a commando quite a few years back and then went downhill from there. Of course, he might have done some sub-agent work for the Commies and overheard something. At any rate, that's irrelevant now. The British need all the help they can get to crack this. I'm sorry, Nick, that you seem to get all the nasty ones, but that goes along with being so good at what you do.'

I acknowledged the compliment. 'Thanks. When do I leave?'

'Early tomorrow morning. It's the first flight out.' He grinned. 'You'll have time to see her again tonight, I should think.'

I grinned back. 'I was counting on it.'

The Miramar Hotel was a pre-colonial vintage building that managed to retain its European flavor. The club was located at the rear of the lobby. I took a table and ordered a scotch on the rocks. When the waiter left with my order, I scanned the surroundings. The room was dimly lit, with most of the illumination coming from the candles which sat atop each table. The clientele was mainly Europeans in Tangier on holiday, with a smattering of modernised Arabs in western garb sipping Turkish coffee, talking animatedly among themselves.

Just as my drink arrived, the lights dimmed and the

show began. The first act was a French singer who went through several numbers bemoaning the heartache of lost loves. She was followed by a procession of belly dancers whose talent was more worthy of Eighth Avenue in New York than the Mid-East.

Finally Hadiya was announced, and a respectful hush settled over the room. The musicians struck up a beat, and Hadiya slid onto the stage from the wings.

She was dressed in the standard belly dancer's costume, but that was as far standard as she was. From the onset it was evident that she was head and shoulders above the average belly dancer. Her abdominal muscles quivered with a control that must have taken years to perfect. Her breasts shook as if they had a mind of their own, and even her arm movements betrayed a grace that was from long ago, when belly dancing was an art rather than the bastardised striptease that it has been relegated to in recent years.

She swirled on bare feet, her body responding to the tempo of the musicians, rising passionately on the upbeats, slowing seductively on the downs. About me I could hear the labored breathing of the male customers as they bent forward to get a better view of her. The few female onlookers glared at her with envy, all the while studying her every movement, trying to copy them for the moment when they could use them in privacy, with their men.

Toward the end of the act the music grew fiercer, but Hadiya kept pace with it, perspiration dripping down her face, following the taut muscles of her neck and disappearing into the deep valley separating her breasts. She reached her peak with a final cresendo of drums, then fell to her knees, her body bent at the waist.

For a minute an awed silence hovered over the room, then, as one, every member of the audience burst into wild applause. Several men stood up, their hands working like pistons – me included. Hadiya acknowledged the applause, then modestly scampered offstage. The hand-clapping gradually subsided, and as if on cue, a collective murmur issued from the customers, each tongue reliving every movement of her act.

I called for my check, paid the waiter and made my way backstage. I was halted in the wings by a burly bouncer who restrained me by placing his meaty hands on my chest. I brushed his hand aside and continued toward the door which, I assumed, was Hadiya's.

I felt the bouncer's heavy hand on my shoulder as I knocked. I was just about to make an argument out of it when Hadiya emerged.

'It's all right, Kassim,' she said, and the grip on my body relaxed. I walked into the dressing room, shutting out the fat Arab.

Hadiya disappeared behind a curtain, changed to street clothing, then walked out the door. When we reached the street, she hailed a taxi and gave the driver the address of her apartment as I settled in next to her.

Hadiya's place was on the top floor of an old, well-kept building in the silversmiths' quarter, overlooking the sea. She opened the door, let me pass, then followed me in and locked it. Light from the full moon poured through the window. I scanned the living room for traces of Fergus. There were none. It was a female's habitat through and through.

Hadiya poured herself a snifter of brandy, handed me one and sat in the only armchair in the room. I sank into the couch and regarded her over the rim of my glass.

Finally I said, 'The photograph Fergus said you should give me?'

She reached into the folds of her dress, and from a pocket pulled the picture. She handed it to me. I studied it. It was an old photograph, faded with time. There were 20 men in it, all wearing desert battle dress, all arranged in a formal group pose of four rows.

'It is Fergus' old commando unit,' Hadiya said. 'He's in the second row, second from the left. It was taken in 1942, in Cairo.'

I turned it to the back, hoping to find something written there. All it bore was the name of the photographer. Whatever Fergus wanted to tell me was in that picture, probably concerning one of the men.

'Tell me about Fergus,' I said.

She sipped her brandy. 'I don't know anything ... about his business, I mean. He was arrested several times for smuggling gold. Once he was questioned by the police about something to do with hashish – I think it was selling it. Other than that, he visited me

31

once, maybe twice, a year. Sometimes he brought me money. Other times he borrowed money from me.'

'The suitcase where the photo came from? What else is in it?'

'Nothing,' she said. 'Just a few old clothes.'

I got up, entered the bedroom. The suitcase lay open on her bed. I rummaged through it, finding nothing but a few changes of men's clothes and an old, moth-eaten wedding dress.

'It was my mother's,' Hadiya said behind me as I held it up.

I turned to her, questioning her with my eyes.

'It was my mother's wedding dress,' she repeated. 'She was Fergus' wife.'

'His what?'

'His wife. She married him when I was four. Fergus was my stepfather.'

Then, for the first time, she betrayed emotion at Fergus' death. Tears flooded her eyes and she buried her head on my chest, her hands clutching my arms. I soothed her the best I could, assuring her that every-thing would be all right. The tears subsided gradually, and she managed to say, 'He was good to me, Nick. He was like my own father. He may have been a bad man, but to me he was good. After my mother died, when I was 10, he cared for me like I was his own daughter.' I nodded, understanding.

We were still standing very close to each other, and suddenly I was aware of a new, different feeling. Hadiya's breasts were pressed against me and I could smell the warm, sweet scent of her hair. My arms moved around her body. I kissed her hard, my tongue snaking into her mouth, exploring it, meeting and entwining with her tongue.

Hadiya reached around behind her and unfastened the buttons of the dress she was wearing. It slipped to her feet. Underneath she wore only tiny sheer black bikini panties that clung to her bronze curves. Her bare breasts which had so excited the tourists at the Miramar a short time earlier thrust outward, full and free, their brown tips erect.

I fumbled for a moment with my own clothing, and then found myself beside that warm, exciting body on the bed. Hadiya's dark eyes glowed softly in the dimness of the room. Her arms pulled me to her and her hands moved down my back.

I kissed her, and now her tongue flicked into my mouth and explored it while her hands caressed me. I laid a row of kisses along her shoulders, moved down to those swelling breasts and finally down across the rise of her belly to the navel that had held a small artificial gem during her dance at the hotel. I lingered at the navel, caressed it with my tongue, and a low moan escaped her.

Her thighs gripped me, and I sought the depths between them. We united with a soft gasp from her. And then those hips that did magic things in the dance began moving in response to my measured thrust. The torrent built inside us. The wild hips thrust and quivered with a primitive rhythm, reaching out for me.

33

She raised her legs high above my shoulders and I gripped her buttocks with both hands. She moaned as she moved in perfect unison with my thrusts, deeper and deeper, harder and harder, trying to lose myself inside her. Hadiya's hips kept moving with me for a long time, but then she arched her back, her fingers raking my arms, a sharp scream coming from her throat. I shuddered, heard myself make a strange animal sound, and collapsed atop her. I was covered with perspiration. I moved off Hadiya. My head sank into the pillow and I dropped off into satisfied sleep.

I was wakened by a tugging at my shoulder. I bolted upright to confront a terrified girl.

'Someone's at the door,' Hadiya hissed in my ear.

I reached for Wilhelmina, but it was too late. The door burst open and a man charged in. He threw a shot my way. I rolled off the bed, landed on the floor. I grasped the night lamp and flung it, then leaped. I hit him just as he was raising his gun to fire again. The palm of my hand swept upward and caught him under his chin. His neck snapped backward with a crack which echoed off the walls of the room.

I reached for the wall switch, turned it on, and looked at the body before me. The man was obviously dying. Then I glanced at Hadiya. A crimson red blotch was spreading below her left breast. She had taken the shot meant for me.

I lifted her head in my hands. Pink bubbles trickled through her lips, then she shivered and was still.

The man on the floor muttered a groan. I went to him. 'Who sent you?' I shook his arm.

'Ayoub,' he coughed, 'my brother . . . ' and he died.

I fished through his pockets, found only a stub from a United Arab Airlines flight. If he was Ayoub's brother, it was natural for him to track me down. Blood vendettas are a part of life in this part of the world. I had killed his brother, and it was his duty to kill me. It was all so damned stupid, and Hadiya was dead because of it.

Two

My BOAC flight 631 arrived at London Airport at
11:05 of a sunny morning the next day. No one met me
because Hawk had not wanted a reception of any kind.
I was to hire a taxi, like any other visitor, and ask the
driver to take me to the British Travel Association
offices at 64 St James Street. There I would see a man
called Brutus. Brutus, his real identity a well-guarded
secret, was Hawk's opposite number in London. He
was the head of Special Operations Executive's Select
Missions Division. He would give me specific instructions regarding the assignment.

I used a password to gain access to the off-limits

top floor of the Travel Association building and was
met by a two-man military guard in spit-and-polish
British Army uniforms. I identified myself.

'Follow us, sir,' one of them told me, deadpan.

We moved down a corridor in close, brisk forma-
tion, the guards' boots pounding in hard rhythm on
the polished floor. We stopped before a large paneled
door at the far end of the corridor.

'You may enter, sir,' the same young man told
me.

'Thank you,' I said and opened the door into a small
reception room.

I closed the door behind me and faced a middle-
aged woman seated behind a desk, evidently Brutus'
secretary. But my eyes traveled quickly past her to a
truly lovely sight. A girl in a very short leather dress,
her back to me, was leaning over a window seat to
water a plant in a box outside the window. Because of
her position, the dress revealed every inch of her long
milky thighs and part of a well-rounded, lace-covered
little behind. I liked Brutus's taste in office help.

The older woman followed my glance. 'Mr Carter, I
presume,' she said, smiling.

'Yes,' I said, reluctantly shifting my gaze. As I
spoke, the girl turned toward us, holding the small
watering can.

'We've been waiting for you,' the secretary said.
'I'm Mrs Smythe and this is Heather York.'

'My pleasure,' I said to Mrs Smythe, but my eyes
returned to the girl. She was blond, her hair cropped

short. Her eyes were large and blue, the most vibrant blue I had ever seen. Her face was perfect: a straight, finely-shaped nose over a wide, sensuous mouth. The micro-mini she was wearing barely covered her even when she was standing straight. The brown leather swelled out over a well-rounded bosom above a narrow waist. Her calves were sheathed in brown boots that matched the dress.

'Brutus will see you immediately, Mr Carter,' said Mrs Smythe. 'The paneled door on your left.'

'Thank you.' I gave the blonde a smile, hoping to see more of her later.

Brutus got up from behind a big mahogany desk as I walked in. 'Well, well! Mr Nick Carter! Good! Good!'

His hand swallowed mine and pumped it. He was a big man, as tall as I, and had one of those square British army faces that is all jaw. There was gray in his sideburns and there were wrinkles around his eyes, but he looked like a man who could still lead a military assault force and enjoy it.

'I'm glad to meet you, sir,' I said.

'My pleasure, my lad! Distinctly my pleasure! Your reputation precedes you, you know.'

I smiled and took the chair he offered me. He didn't go back to his seat but stood at one corner of the desk, his expression suddenly somber.

'We've got a big one here, Nick,' he said. 'I'm sorry to get you involved in our problems, but you're not well known here for one thing and, frankly, I wanted an experienced man who would have no hesitancy about killing, if it becomes necessary. Our only man of your caliber is inextricably involved in a problem at Malta.'

'I'm glad to help,' I said.

I gave him the details of all that had happened in Egypt, then surrendered the photograph. He studied it for a while, then agreed with me that whatever Fergus wanted to tell us had something to do with one or several of the men in the snapshot.

'It will take time to track all these men down,' he said. 'Meanwhile, there is still Novosty.'

Brutus began pacing beside the desk, his hands behind his back. 'We don't know whether this is the Commies or not. We know Novosty is here for some sinister purpose but it may have nothing to do with the assassinations. We have to check him out, though, and time is vital. If you get any other ideas, explore them. Just be sure to check with me regularly.'

He reached over his desk, picked up two slips of paper and handed them to me. They were the original notes left by the assassin or assassins. I studied them.

'You'll notice they're both handwritten and by the same person,' Brutus pointed out.

'Yes,' I said pensively. 'Have you had the writing analysed?'

'No,' he said, 'but I can arrange it if you like.'

I nodded. I was no expert but the scrawling style didn't suggest a cool professional agent to me. Of

40

course, that could be part of the smokescreen. 'Hawk said the killings were bloody.'

Brutus sighed and dropped into the leather chair behind the desk. 'Yes. You understand, we've tried to keep the messier details out of the papers. Wellsey had the back of his head blown off with a high-powered rifle. He was shot through his office window by an expert marksman at some distance. Almost suggestive of a professional hunter.'

'Or a professional killer,' I said.

'Yes.' He rubbed his chin. 'The Percy Dumbarton killing was quite nasty. He was stabbed while out walking his dog. The dog's throat was cut too. The note was pinned to Dumbarton's coat. The first note, by the way, was found in the unopened mail on Wellsey's desk.'

'Maybe you should just pay the money and see what happens,' I suggested.

'We've thought of that. But twelve million pounds sterling is a lot of money even to the British government. I'll tell you frankly, though, there is considerable pressure from the cabinet people and the ministry to pay, nevertheless. We may wind up doing just that. But, for the moment, you have at least a week to develop something.'

'I'll do my best, sir.'

'I know you generally prefer to work alone,' Brutus said, 'but I'm going to assign an agent from my SM Division to work with you on this. The two of you will report *only* to me. There are other agencies working on this, naturally – MI5, MI6, the Yard and others. They are not to share in any information you develop except through me. Is that understood?'

'Completely,' I told him.

He smiled. 'Good.' He pushed a button on his desk. 'Send York in, Miss Smythe.'

I frowned. Wasn't that the name of the blonde I'd been introduced to in the outer office . . .? The door behind me opened and I turned. The lovely creature in the leather micro-mini moved briskly into the room, giving me a big smile as she walked past me to the mahogany desk. She sat on the edge of the desk as if she'd perched there many times before.

'This is Mr Nick Carter, Heather,' Brutus said, smiling at her. 'Nick, Miss Heather York.'

'We met outside,' she said, not taking her eyes off me.

'Oh, good.' He looked at me. 'Heather is the agent you'll be working with, Nick.'

I looked from the girl to Brutus and back to her. 'I'll be damned,' I said softly.

After filling Heather in about the photograph, Brutus dismissed us. As I reached the door, he said, 'Keep in touch. We should have something on the men in the picture in a day or so.'

I took a cab to a small hotel near Russell Square, having recovered slightly from the pleasant shock of finding I was to spend the next week or so with a bundle of goodies like Heather York. Actually, I had mixed feelings about her. Women and espionage don't mix, not the way I play the game. And it was difficult for me to believe that such an exquisite package as Heather could be of much real help finding an assassin. But Brutus was the boss during this lend-lease assignment and I wasn't about to question his judgment.

My orders were to stick pretty close to the hotel during the next few hours while Heather made preparations for us to drive to Cornwall later in the day. The cab driver took me along Pall Mall, past the National Gallery at Trafalgar Square where the tourists were feeding the pigeons at Nelson's Column in the sunshine.

We were coming to the park at Russell Square. The hotel was only a couple of blocks away and I felt like walking a little.

'I'll get out here,' I told the driver.

'Right, governor,' the man said, slowing the cab.

I paid him and he drove off. I walked past the park, enjoying the autumn sunshine, and finally turned down the side street toward my hotel. A lone black Austin sat at the curb up ahead. As I came up to it, I saw there were three men in dark suits inside. Two of them got out and confronted me, blocking my way.

'Excuse me, old chap, but would you be Mr Carter, by any chance?'

I studied the man. He was a square, blocky young guy. He looked like a cop . . . or security agent. So did his buddy, especially with his right hand snuggled in his jacket pocket.

'What if I am?' I said.

'Then we would be wanting a chat with you,' the blocky young man said with a tight grin. 'Come along, we don't want to worry anyone, do we?'

I glanced around. There was always someone around the park at Russell Square, but the side streets were often deserted. Right now there were only a couple of people on the street and walking in the opposite direction. No help there.

'Get in, Mr Carter.' The order came from the third man, the driver, and I felt something hard shoved into my back. 'Search him first,' he told his pals, leaning out of the window.

The first man reached inside my jacket and removed Wilhelmina from her holster. He stuck the Luger into his belt, then he patted me down. He did a sloppy job, missing both Hugo on my right forearm and Pierre, the cyanide gas bomb, taped to my inner left thigh.

'Get in the car, Mr Carter,' he said. 'We want to know what dealings you had with Augie Fergus before he died.'

'Who is "we"?'

'A man named Novosty,' the first one said.

'So that's it,' I said.

'That's it, Yank,' the second man told me, speaking for the first time.

'Take me to him, then,' I said. I don't argue with guns staring me in the face.

The second man uttered a harsh laugh. 'You'd like that, wouldn't you? But it is not going to be so easy.

You'll just come with us, tell us what we want to know, then take the next plane back to America.'

I climbed into the back seat and they got in after me, one on each side. They were taking no chances. We pulled away from the curb.

We were heading along Oxford Street now, toward Marble Arch. If they stayed on that main street, it would complicate things. Just before we reached Hyde Park, though, the driver turned into a narrow side street, heading toward Grosvenor Square. This was my chance, if there was ever going to be one.

The man on my left was watching the progress of the car, but his buddy with the gun hadn't taken his eyes – or the gun – off me. So I had to encourage him a little.

'Look out!' I said suddenly. 'In the street there.'

The driver slowed automatically and the two men in in the back seat looked forward for a split second. That was all I needed. I chopped down hard on the gun arm of the agent on my right and the gun dropped to the floor of the car. I followed that up with a quick, hard chop to his throat that left him gagging.

The other agent was grabbing for my arm. I jerked free and rammed the elbow savagely into his face, breaking his nose. He grunted and collapsed into the corner.

The Austin careered wildly along the narrow street as the driver tried to steer with one hand and point his gun at me with the other. 'Stop it, Carter! Stop it, you bloody bastard.'

I pushed the gun toward the roof of the car, twisted the wrist and the gun went crashing through a side window, splintering glass. I felt a sharp pain in my right cheek where a piece of flying glass stabbed me.

The driver had completely lost control of the Austin now. It skidded from one side of the street to the other, passed gaping pedestrians, finally going up over the right curb and crashing into a utility pole. The driver's head struck the windshield and he collapsed against the wheel.

Retrieving Wilhelmina from the man on my left, I reached over the agent on my right and kicked the door on that side. It sprang open and I threw myself over the man and through the door, hitting the pavement on my shoulder and rolling with the impact.

I got up and looked around at the Austin, at the two dazed men in the back and the unconscious driver slumped over the steering wheel.

'Don't bother to drive me back,' I said.

Three

'Since time is so important,' Heather York was saying across the intimacy of a table for two, 'Brutus insisted we leave for Cornwall this evening. Actually, I rather like driving at night.'

She was wearing a short, very short, green dress with shoes to match and an auburn wig styled in a shoulder-length hairdo. I told her when she picked me up at the hotel, 'If that wig's supposed to be a disguise, it won't work – I'd know that figure anywhere.'

She laughed, shaking her head. 'No disguise, a girl just likes to change her personality once in a while.'

On the way to the little restaurant on the outskirts of London, where we stopped for dinner before proceeding south to the coast, I described my run-in with Novosty's boys.

She chuckled. 'Brutus must have loved that ... you did call him?'

'I did.'

The restaurant was charming, very Old English. The waiters had just brought our order when a man approached the table. He was tall and square with blond hair and a rugged face. Along the left side of his neck, almost hidden by his shirt, was a thin scar. He had hard dark brown eyes.

'Heather – Heather York?' he said as he stopped at the table. 'Yes! I almost missed you with the wig. Very flattering.'

Heather responded with a strained smile. 'Elmo Jupiter! Nice to see you again.'

'I was going to ask you and your friend to join us,' he motioned toward a dark-haired girl at a table in the corner, 'but I see you've been served.'

'Yes,' Heather said. 'This is Richard Matthews ... Elmo Jupiter, Richard.'

I nodded. 'My pleasure.'

He studied me for a moment and the hard eyes were definitely hostile. 'You're an American.'

'Yes.'

'Heather does have exotic tastes.' He grinned, turning back to her. 'In men and motorcars. Well, I must get back to my black ale. I'll see you about, Heather.'

'Yes, of course,' she said, still wearing the tight smile. 'Have a good evening.'

'I always do,' Jupiter said, turning away.

As he walked back to his table, Heather glanced at the girl waiting for him there. 'I don't like that man,' she said abruptly. 'I met him through a friend who's a clerk at SOE. He thinks I work in public health. He asked me out but I made an excuse. I don't like his eyes.'

'I think he's jealous,' I said.

'He probably resents my turning him down. He's used to getting what he wants, I hear. Makes automobiles, I believe. He'd be surprised to learn about the girl he's with. She has a long record for selling drugs.'

'How do you know that?' I asked.

'I worked at the Yard for almost a year before SOE offered me my job.'

She said it casually, as if it were of no importance, but I was impressed. Lovely Heather, I suspected, was full of surprises.

We drove all that evening and into the night along winding, shrub-lined narrow roads at first, passing through villages with such names as Crownhill and Moorswater, then along the seacoast for a while. Heather drove her dated but custom-made S.O.C.E. M.A. Gregoire.

'It has a Ferodo type 11L clutch,' she told me proudly as we roared around a tortuous curve in the blackness, the headlights scything two swaths of yellow through the night. She had abandoned the wig and her short blond hair was mussed by the wind. 'And a Cotal type MK electromagnetic gearbox.'

We stopped at a bed-and-breakfast inn long after midnight when Heather finally tired of driving. She asked for separate rooms. When we were given adjoining rooms and a wink by the old Scottish landlord, Heather offered no objection but no encouragement either. So I fell asleep in my own bed, trying not to think of her so close.

We arrived very early in Penzance where Novosty was reported to have been seen a couple of days before. Brutus had given us a detailed description of him and what was known of his cover. He was going under the name of John Ryder and his English was supposed to be flawless.

After some discreet inquiries at the local hotels and pubs, we learned that a man answering Novosty's description had indeed been in Penzance, at the Queens Hotel, with another man. He and his companion had checked out of the hotel the previous morning, but the desk clerk had overheard Novosty mention Land's End, the tip of Cornwall jutting into the sea.

'It's Land's End then,' Heather said as we drove out of town. 'A perfect place to hide and plot.'

'Maybe,' I said. 'But we go slow from now on. Novosty probably knows we're looking for him.'

'You're the boss.' She smiled.

The road to Land's End was a bleak one, winding over rocky terrain dotted with heather and gorse, and passing through gray stone villages. About five miles from our destination, we stopped a farmer driving a wagon in the opposite direction and asked about visitors to the neighborhood.

He rubbed his ruddy cheeks with a thick hand. 'Two gentlemen took up in the Heamoor cottage yesterday. The one chap give me a fiver for priming the well. Seemed nice enough gents.'

The stench of manure rose from the wagon. Heather wrinkled her nose and gave me a smile.

'That wouldn't be our chap,' I lied. 'The man we're looking for is here with his family. Thanks, anyway.'

The farmer flicked his horse into motion and we drove off slowly. When the wagon was out of sight, we took the first turn in the direction the farmer had indicated. About a hundred yards along the dirt road, I motioned for Heather to pull over to the side.

'The cottage can't be far,' I said. 'We'll walk the rest of the way.'

A bird called out in irritation from the field beside us as we got out of the car. Otherwise the morning was sunny and silent. We followed the winding road for a couple hundred more yards before we saw the cottage.

I pushed Heather down behind some tall grass. 'That must be it,' I whispered.

The brown stone cottage squatted on a low hill covered with gorse, the yellow blossoms giving some relief to the stark scene. Parked beside the cottage was a small blue Sunbeam sedan. There had been no attempt to hide the car from the road. Apparently

51

Novosty thought he was safe from observation – or else he wanted others to think he did.

I touched Heather's arm and indicated that we would circle around to the side of the cottage where we could approach it behind the cover of the car. I started off through the grass, Heather following.

As we crawled up to the parked Sunbeam, we could hear voices. There was a window open on that side of the cottage. I reached into my jacket for Wilhelmina and Heather took a small Sterling .380 PPL automatic out of her purse. I motioned for her to stay put and cover me. Slowly I crawled to the side of the cottage, stopped underneath the window.

The voices were very distinct now. I straightened up as high as the window ledge and took a quick glance inside. There were three men in the cottage: a tall, thin man with light brown hair and a bony face – Novosty apparently – was striding around the room speaking to two other men who looked British. I ducked back down and listened.

'When we return to London there will be no further contact except by prearranged dead-drop message,' Novosty was saying. 'Above all, none of us must be seen at the Defence Ministry prior to our target date. Is that understood?'

There was a mumbling of assent from the others.

'Good. On the target date, there will be a heavy guard at the Ministry. Our timing must be very nearly perfect. Our subject will be exposed to us for only seconds. We must make our move swiftly and efficiently.'

'Don't worry about us, mate,' one of the Englishmen said cooly.

'We'll give them a bleeding good show,' his companion agreed.

Novosty lowered his voice. I leaned forward to get in a better position to hear him when there was a sound at the back of the cottage. Heather's whisper reached me almost simultaneously.

'Nick! Look out!'

It was too late. A stocky man came around the side of the cottage from the rear, carrying a pail of water. He had apparently been to the well out back. When he saw me, he swore in Russian and dropped the pail. He fit the description I had been given of a resident KGB operator for southern England. Spotting Wilhelmina, he reached desperately into his hip pocket for his own gun.

I aimed and fired the Luger in one motion; the shot echoed loudly in the quiet morning. The Russian grabbed at his chest and the gun he had pulled out went flying against the wall of the cottage. The KGB man stumbled backwards, landed spread-legged in the gorse, his hands clutching at empty air.

'Run for the tall grass!' I shouted at Heather. Then, without waiting for an acknowledgment, I ran headlong for the back of the cottage, hoping there was a door there.

I almost stumbled over the dropped pail as I

rounded the corner. I saw the door, closed. I kicked out at it savagely and it crashed inward.

As I moved into the cottage, into a room behind the one where Novosty and the others had been talking, one of the Englishmen came through an open doorway, holding a Webley 455 Mark IV, and ran into me without breaking stride. His face reflected surprise as we hit. He was knocked back against the door jamb, time enough for me to aim Wilhelmina and open a hole in his gut. He slumped to the floor, eyes open, the surprised look still on his face.

I moved on into the front room of the cottage but it was empty. Then I heard shots from out front. Novosty and the other man were outside, exchanging fire with Heather. She was apparently keeping them away from the blue sedan with her small pistol. I started toward the front door, planning to come up behind them, when the second Briton came charging back into the cottage.

He fired first but the shot was wild. My Luger exploded twice and both shots scored. I didn't stop to watch him fall. There was a rapid exchange of gunfire outside and then I heard a car door slam. A second later, the engine roared. As I stepped out of the cottage, the Sunbeam skidded off across the open ground, heading for the road.

I could just barely see the top of Novosty's head as he crouched low over the wheel to avoid Heather's fire. Resting Wilhelmina on my forearm, I sighted along the barrel and aimed for the right rear tire. But just as I fired, the sedan bounced in and out of a rut, veering crazily. The shot missed the tire and dug up dirt instead. Then the car was gone down the road, hidden by high grass.

I dropped Wilhelmina to my side and sighed. The one man we really wanted had gotten away. He could find other agents within days, maybe even hours. And if Novosty was the assassin, we probably hadn't even slowed him down.

I remembered Heather then and turned toward the high brush. I found her reloading the Sterling PPL.

'Sorry he got past me,' she apologised.

'Couldn't be helped,' I said.

'I suppose there's little point in trying to follow him in my car.'

'He's got too big a start on us,' I said.

'Yes.' She sounded depressed.

'Are you okay?'

'Yes. I'm all right. And you?'

'The best of health,' I told her. 'I can't say the same for those two in there.' I motioned toward the cottage.

We searched the two Britons and the cottage but found nothing. Then I went through the pockets of the dead KGB man. Nothing. Novosty was a real pro – with the pro's aversion to writing anything down.

'They were talking about the Defence Ministry,' I told Heather. 'They were definitely planning something there.

'Novosty talked about "our subject" and "target date" and said they had to "make their move swiftly."

Novosty could be our man. We'd better presume that he is, and that he plans to kill again soon. If it's part of a grand plan, he'll just change time, date and method of operation for the next attempt.'

'The Defence Ministry,' Heather mused. 'With Dumbarton already assassinated, who does that leave? His second in command?'

'Maybe, or maybe a general. Who knows?' I said. I was going through one of the dead men's wallet for the second time. I noticed a secret compartment I had missed the first time. Inside was a slip of paper. I pulled it out. 'Hey! What's this?'

Heather looked over my shoulder. 'It's a telephone number.'

'What's that written under it?'

She took it from me. 'Lower Slaughter.'

'Lower . . . What in the world is that?'

She looked up at me, her blue eyes smiling. 'It's a town, a small village in the Cotswolds. This must be a number in the village.'

'Well,' I said thoughtfully, 'maybe one of Novosty's boys made a small mistake.'

Four

'And the second note?' I asked, the phone cradled to my ear, photostatic copies of the assassination notes Brutus had made up for me spread out on the bed beside me. 'Were there any differences?'

I was speaking to the graphoanalyst Brutus had given the assassination notes to. I listened intently to his reply.

'Well,' I said as he finished, 'I appreciate your help.'

I hung up and turned to Heather, who sat on the other of the twin beds. We had registered at this Stratford hotel as husband and wife – at her suggestion.

'That's interesting,' I said.

'What?' she asked.

I studied the photostats pensively. I had circled certain letters as I listened to the handwriting expert.

'Take a look at this,' I told Heather. 'Notice how the letters all slant at a sharp angle to the right side of the paper. The graphologist feels it means the writer is a very emotional person, possibly a disturbed personality.'

'But our dossier on Novosty shows him to be a cool, systematic and efficient agent,' Heather protested. 'His records at Gaczyna all tell the same story.' She was referring to stolen records from the Soviet spy school.

'Exactly. Now, look at the open A's and O's in this first note. A careful, precise man like Novosty would close those letters at the top.

'Secretive persons always close their O's,' I continued. 'And there's more. See how the T is crossed in "Britain"? A strong, firm crossing line through the body of the letter, indicating a strength bordering on stubbornness and undue aggressiveness. Again, Novosty doesn't fit the pattern. Then, there's the hurried style of writing, suggesting irritability and impatience. Can you see the Soviets picking an impatient man for a master spy?'

Heather smiled. 'I rather wish they would.'

I returned the smile. 'That's not our luck, I'm afraid.' I looked back down at the photostats and stopped smiling as I compared them. 'Last but not least there's a pronounced slant downward to the lines in these notes. It's most evident in the second note. That shows the writer is seething with emotion, full of depressions and anxieties.'

Heather regarded the notes ruefully. 'A man like that would be found out very quickly in the KGB.'

'And given a quick discharge,' I agreed.

'Blimey!' Heather breathed, in one of her rare lapses into street slang. 'It's a ruddy guessing game, it is!'

'With time running out on us,' I added. 'In a few days, there will be another assassination.'

'What do we do now?' She crossed her long legs, showing a flash of lace under the yellow mini dress she was wearing. She looked like a schoolgirl, wondering if she had passed an exam. But she had not behaved like a schoolgirl out there at the cottage at Land's End.

'We go on to Lower Slaughter and try to relocate Novosty while there is still time. Maybe all that phone number is is a lead to somebody's girlfriend. But it could be Novosty's real headquarters. I just hope it's not a dead end.'

In the morning we drove to Lower Slaughter along narrow roads, passing thatched-roofed, black and white cottages and signs directing the traveler to such places as Chipping Campden and Bourton-on-the-Water. Lower Slaughter itself was a serene old tree-shaded village of brown stone cottages with a stream running through it. We parked the car on a side street and walked to the address Brutus's research department had traced through the telephone number we'd given them. It was a small house on the edge of town and it appeared to be deserted. There was no blue sedan around and the door was locked.

We moved around to the back and I looked in through a small leaded-glass window. I saw no one. I took an adjustable key from my pocket, one of the many devices provided by Hawk's Special Effects and Editing boys, and manipulated the lock with it. In a moment, a tumbler clicked and the door opened. I pulled Wilhelmina out and stepped cautiously inside. I moved slowly through a rustic kitchen into a living room, then into a bedroom. When I returned to the living room, Heather was checking the house out for 'bugs.' There were none.

I had just about decided that there was little point in hanging around when I found the overnight case stashed in a small closet. It had all the necessary male toilet articles in it, and they had been recently used. I looked around some more and spotted a crumpled but fresh cigarette butt in a wastebasket. The cigarette was one of the three British brands preferred by Russians and other East Europeans.

'Novosty beat us here,' I told Heather. 'And he'll be back.'

'Yes,' she said, 'and he's already had company.' She showed me two liqueur glasses she had found in a kitchen cupboard, recently used and left unwashed.

I smiled, leaned down and brushed her cheek with

my lips. 'Very good,' I said. She looked at me as if she wanted more, then quickly looked around. I had a difficult time remembering what I was there for.

'There is a man named Koval,' Heather said, her eyes on the glasses she was holding. 'He's a Russian agent who has been seen in this area and who has a liking for this type of liqueur. Stanislas Koval.'

'Apparently he's Novosty's new subordinate,' I said. 'They may be out recruiting more agents right now.'

'Koval would be able to call on a number of men he has already cleared,' Heather said.

'That's right. But we have a small advantage now. We're here and they don't know it.'

Heather was wearing a corduroy skirt and one of those braless jersey shirts – I could see the contours of her nipples through the clinging material. It was no different from what all the other girls were wearing in the new days of female emancipation, but on Heather – and under the circumstances – it was distracting and frustrating. I think she knew it bothered me and was rather enjoying it. I tore my eyes away from those nipples and went to the kitchen to relock the back door. Then I replaced the overnight case and cigarette butt while Heather put the dirty glasses back into the cupboard where she had found them.

'Now,' I said, 'we'll wait.' Deliberately I let my gaze travel over the jersey blouse and down to where the short corduroy skirt stopped at mid-thigh. 'Do you have any suggestions as to where?'

She gave me just a hint of a smile. 'The bedroom?'
I returned her smile. 'Of course,' I said.

We moved into the bedroom and closed the door.
Heather went to the one window and looked outside.
'Very quiet out there,' she said, turning back to me
and tossing her purse on the bed. 'We just may have
ourselves a long wait.'

'We just might, and I don't propose to waste it.'

I moved close to her, circled her waist with my hand
and started to draw her to me. She arched her back so
that the soft curves of her pressed against me.

'I've been looking forward to this,' I said, placing a
kiss on her neck just under the blond hair.

'I've been wanting you ever since you walked into
Brutus's office,' she whispered back.

She helped me off with my jacket and Wilhelmina
and then my shirt. I was undoing the catch that held
her skirt up. In a moment it dropped to the floor. She
stood there in sheer lace panties, all willowy curves
and softness, her skin milky white and smooth as
velvet.

'We can't use the bed,' I said, watching her slide the
panties over her hips. I removed the rest of my clothes
and drew her down beside me on the bedroom rug.

I pressed her back onto the floor and kissed her.
She responded eagerly, moving her hips against me in
gentle undulating movements. I caressed her as I
kissed her and felt her thighs part at my touch. Obviously, she was in no mood to waste time either. Gently,
I covered her body with mine.

I entered her in one smooth, flowing motion. Her hands were doing magical things on my back, moving lower and lower, caressing, fondling, exciting me more and more. I started to move quicker, and I could feel Heather respond. Her legs parted wider as if she wanted me as deeply inside her as I could possibly go. Her breath came in rasping sobs. I thrust farther into her and she moaned as we climaxed together, perfectly.

Afterwards, we dressed slowly. When Heather had pulled on the jersey again, I leaned over and kissed her lightly on the lips.

'We're going to have to make a custom of this lend-lease business,' I said.

'I'll see what Brutus can arrange.' She smiled.

We hadn't been dressed for long when I heard a car stopping. Heather was in the kitchen. I moved quickly to the bedroom window, pulling my jacket on. A black sedan had pulled up in front of the house. There were three men in it. One of them was Novosty.

I rushed to the bedroom door as Novosty and his pals got out of the car and moved toward the house. 'Heather!' I whispered harshly. 'They're here!'

A key scraped in the lock. Heather was nowhere in sight. I ducked back into the bedroom as the front door opened.

Five

'It is possible I can get someone else besides Marsh here,' one of the men was saying as the three entered. I glimpsed a heavyset, curly-haired character carrying a bag of groceries. He moved through the front room to the kitchen and I figured him for Koval. 'But you understand that this is very short notice.'

I held my breath as Koval entered the kitchen. Heather was in there somewhere. Maybe she had managed to slip into the pantry. I could hear the curly-haired man moving about the kitchen.

'You can tell that to the Kremlin, Comrade.' It was Novosty, and it was said with heavy sarcasm. I saw him as he sat down in a chair near the doorway. I eased the door shut, leaving just a half-inch slit. Heather's purse, I noticed out of the corner of my eyes, wasn't on the bed anymore. Had she taken it with her . . . ? And then I saw it in the far corner by the bed where it must have fallen somehow. Her Sterling automatic would be in it.

I set my jaw in frustration. Heather was unarmed and we were separated. It had been rotten timing.

A tall angular Briton with a neat mustache moved to a couch near Novosty.

'I know a chap what might work out,' he told the Russian. 'Harry the Ape, they call him. A right sort he is for a bashing fracas. He's keen on a fight of any kind.'

Novosty's voice betrayed impatience. 'We can't use ordinary hoodlums in this operation, Marsh. We need men with good heads or the mission will fail.'

'Right enough,' the Briton said, unperturbed.

Koval stuck his head in from the kitchen. 'A glass of vodka, Comrades?'

'I'll give it a go,' Marsh said.

'Yes, please.' Novosty nodded. He rose, took off his jacket – and headed straight for the bedroom.

I made a dash for the closet. Just as I pulled the door closed, Novosty entered the room and threw his jacket on the bed. He pulled his tie off and for a moment I thought he was coming to the closet with it. I had Wilhelmina out and ready to fire if he opened the door. But he turned short of the closet and slipped out of my field of vision for a moment, apparently hanging the tie on some hook on the wall. He had been three feet from a 9mm slug in the chest. In another moment, he left the room.

I hadn't had time to leave the closet when I heard a commotion from the kitchen. Koval exclaimed loudly in Russian, and then there was a crash. He had found Heather. Seconds later, she screamed.

I slammed the closet door open and rushed into the living room. Novosty heard me coming and was waiting for me. Metal slammed against my skull and I saw Novosty's arm and the gun butt that had hit me as I went down, pain ricocheting in my head.

I fired Wilhelmina automatically, but the slug only splintered wood behind Novosty's head. As I hit the floor I almost lost the Luger, but I held on grimly while my legs grabbed for purchase. I had Wilhelmina aimed for a second shot when Marsh's big fist rammed my face. The impact knocked me flat and this time I did lose the Luger.

'Try not to kill either of them!' Novosty called out. There was another crash from the kitchen and a yell from Koval. Heather was keeping him busy. But I was in big trouble of my own. Marsh had moved over me now, waiting for me to get up. I chopped at his leg, connected with his shin, and he cried out. I grabbed his foot, pulled hard and he hit the floor beside me.

I got my feet under me finally. My head was spinning, but as Marsh struggled up, I grabbed him by the lapels, turned with him in a half circle and flung him against Novosty, just as the Russian was aiming his snub-nosed automatic at me. Marsh knocked Novosty back over a table and both men crashed to the floor.

I started toward them but this time Novosty was too quick for me.

'Stay where you are!' The Russian was up on one knee, the automatic pointed at my chest. I had little choice; Hugo the stiletto could not be brought into play fast enough.

'Anything you say,' I said.

Koval emerged from the kitchen at that point, holding Heather.

'Well,' Novosty said with obvious satisfaction, 'our two friends from Land's End. It is a pleasure to meet you again.'

'I wish I could say the feeling is mutual,' I said.

Marsh now staggered back to his feet.

'Go wash your face off,' Novosty told him. 'Koval, tie these two up.'

Koval grunted. He released Heather and disappeared into the kitchen again while Novosty held the gun carefully on us. In a minute, Koval was back. He tied my hands behind me with a length of strong rope. Then he tied Heather. Novosty had us sitting on the old flower-patterned sofa in the middle of the room by the time Marsh returned, his face washed and a couple of strips of adhesive across his cuts. He glowered at me.

Novosty brought a chair up near us and sat down. He lighted a cigarette, the brand we had found in the waste-basket.

'Now,' he said, blowing smoke toward my face. 'Do you work for MI5?'

The rules are that you never tell the enemy anything he doesn't know already even if it seems insignificant at the time. Novosty knew this but he had to ask.

'We're with Scotland Yard,' Heather said coolly. 'You're moving drugs, aren't you?'

Novosty laughed. 'Oh, really,' he said. 'You can do better than that, I'm sure.'

Heather's face remained expressionless. She seemed not to have been badly hurt in her fight with Koval, I was relieved to see. Novosty turned to me.

'And what is your story?' he asked.

I looked into those flat eyes and wondered again how this man could be our killer. Novosty could kill all right and undoubtedly had that very thing in mind for us. But he would do it coldly and ruthlessly and without emotion because it was a job that had to be done. There would be no remorse in it, but no real pleasure either. He was a professional.

'I don't have a story,' I told him.

Novosty smiled an easy smile and took a gentlemanly drag on the long cigarette. Again he blew the smoke towards me. 'The girl is MI5,' he said smoothly. 'No, wait. SOE. I recall a dossier. And you with your American accent. A ruse maybe, or are you on loan from the Americans?'

Novosty was smart. I leaned back against the sofa and glared at him. 'You figure it out.'

He shrugged. 'It makes little difference which

agency you're working for,' he said lightly.

'Let Marsh work on him,' Koval suggested.

'Yeah, I'll give the bleeding bloke something to think about,' Marsh growled.

'You see how eager my friends are?' Novosty grinned at me. 'It would be well for you to consider cooperating.'

'I told you!' Heather said. 'We're undercover policemen. Why don't you just show us where the heroin is and cop a plea? We'll recommend leniency at the Yard.'

Novosty shook his head, smiling. 'You have an imaginative colleague,' he said to me. 'But not a very realistic one, I'm afraid.' The smile faded. He leaned over and carefully squashed the cigarette in an ashtray. When his eyes met mine again, he meant business.

'I know you killed one man at Land's End. What about the other two? Did you kill them too or are you holding them for interrogation?'

'No comment,' I said.

He nodded to Marsh; the big Englishman slugged me across the mouth with his open hand. My head snapped back so hard, I thought for a moment he might have broken my neck. Blood ran from the corner of my mouth. I saw Heather watching anxiously.

'Well?' Novosty said. 'What did you overhear at the cottage? Are any of our friends there alive and what have they told you?'

I sat and stared at him, conscious of the blood trickling down to my chin. Novosty looked at Marsh, and the big hand came at me again, this time balled into a fist. The blow knocked me on to my side on the sofa. I lay there for a moment, groggy, and then the big hands pulled me back to a sitting position.

'I don't like to do this,' Novosty said, 'but you give me little choice. How long were you at the window of the cottage before our friend saw you?'

I licked swollen lips. 'What window?' I said.

Novosty's eyes narrowed. 'So that is the way it is going to be.'

Koval moved closer to Novosty. 'Let Marsh work on the girl,' he said quietly. He jerked his head at me. 'He likes her – I can tell.'

'All right,' Novosty said. 'But start off mildly. We want to know what they've learned.'

'Perhaps quite mildly, eh?' Koval said. He nodded at Heather's long and lovely legs.

Novosty waved a hand. 'Whatever you wish.'

Koval gave Marsh a look, and Marsh put on a big grin. He moved over to Heather and pulled her to her feet. Koval held her while Marsh untied her hands. Koval ran a fat hand over her breasts, slowly, grinning now. Heather hauled off and slapped his face.

Koval responded by slapping her back, hard. She would have lost her footing if Marsh hadn't been holding her. Her face was red from the blow.

I set my jaw and tried not to watch. It was going to get worse before it got better. But if they found out that we knew about the Defence Ministry, we would have lost the only advantage we had.

Koval and Marsh were wrestling Heather's clothing off. She fought them as best she could, grunting but otherwise silent. In a moment, she was naked. Marsh held her while Koval ran those pudgy hands of his over her very slowly. Novosty looked bored.

'Leave the girl alone,' I said. 'She knows nothing. Neither do I. I arrived at your damned window too late to hear anything.'

Novosty eyed me narrowly, appraising what I had said. 'That undoubtedly means you know everything or most of it. Now, save the girl further problems by telling me who you have passed this information on to. Have you managed to reach your headquarters?'

'We found out nothing,' I said. 'We have nothing to tell.'

Novosty studied my bruised and bloody face and nodded to Koval. Marsh threw Heather bodily to the floor in front of me; he and Koval both watched my reaction. Koval held Heather's arms above her head.

'You want to see your girl friend raped?' he said. 'How would you like that? She's a lovely thing, isn't she?'

Marsh grinned and licked his lips. Just looking at him made me sick. I didn't want to look at Heather.

I hesitated. Was it worth going on with this? How much, actually, did we have to gain by playing dumb? We were protecting little information. On the other hand, by admitting what we knew and bluffing a little to boot, we might at least find out if Novosty and his crew were an assassin team or if they were up to some other game altogether.

'Okay, I'll tell you what you want to know,' I said. 'Let the girl go.'

'I hope you're not playing games again,' Novosty said.

Marsh glared in frustration, but Koval gave him a look that said there would be plenty of time for such things later, before they killed Heather. Koval released her arms and she sat up, trying to cover her nakedness with her hands.

'Take the girl into the bedroom. Give her her clothes,' Novosty said. 'You do it, Koval. Marsh, you stay here.'

Heather looked at me questioningly as she moved past me to the bedroom, holding her clothes against her. Koval followed and closed the door. I remember Heather's purse then and wondered if she'd have a chance to get to it – and her little gun – before Koval saw it.

'Now, my friend,' Novosty said. 'We will talk business. First, what dealings did you have with Augie Fergus in Egypt?'

'He was going to sell me some information. But he was killed by his Arab friends before he could give it.'

'And what was this information?'

'He didn't say,' I lied. 'But what was Fergus to you?'

'Nothing,' Novosty sneered. 'Just a man who did

jobs for us now and then in the Mid-East. Our people there asked me to find out about your dealings with him. Now, about the comrades at Land's End. Are they dead?'

'They're dead,' I said.

'And they told you nothing?'

'Nothing. I overheard you talking through the window, though, before your Russian friend spotted me. About the Defence Ministry.'

Novosty's face went blank. 'I see.'

I was thinking as I talked. They had not removed my jacket and, when Koval frisked me, he had not found Hugo. But I couldn't use the stiletto as long as my hands were tied behind my back.

'I understand you plan to execute your mission as your man leaves the building.' I watched Novosty's face; it remained expressionless.

'What exactly is our mission?'

I hesitated, watching him and Marsh; I wanted to see both their reactions to what I was about to say. 'Why, to assassinate a third British government official,' I said, 'in accordance with your overall plan.'

Novosty's eyes narrowed slightly, the only change of expression. But Marsh was a different story. His eyebrows went up in surprise and he barked a laugh. Novosty gave him a hard look but Marsh's laugh had told me plenty. At least, he thought the mission he'd been recruited for was something quite different.

'We did not speak of assassination at Land's End,'

Novosty said. 'Are you playing a last hand with me?'

'I didn't actually hear the word,' I admitted. 'But we've known for some time now that this supposed attempt to blackmail the British government is actually a series of planned executions for Russia's benefit. It's a Soviet plot and you were sent here to see it through.'

I watched Novosty's face and he watched mine. It was like playing draw poker, except that the stakes were our lives – mine and Heather's – and Britain's security.

'But you do not know who we plan to kill next,' Novosty said thoughtfully.

'No, it can be one of several possible targets. We don't know the exact date either but that won't help you much. The game is up, and Russia will soon be exposed.' I raised my voice, letting a little emotion slip in. Watching Novosty, I concluded that he believed me. But he wasn't about to deny the charge, not just yet.

'Take him to the bedroom,' he told Marsh with no further comment on what I'd told him. 'Tie the girl again and lock the shutters on the window. Then bring Koval back out with you.'

Marsh took me into the bedroom where Koval was watching Heather. The Russian had found Heather's purse, I noticed, which was a disappointment. They locked the window and tied Heather's hands behind her. As Marsh left the room, he punched a big fist into my stomach. I grunted and doubled over, going to my knees. Marsh laughed and followed Koval out of the room. The door closed behind them.

I couldn't breath for a long, agonising moment. Heather knelt awkwardly beside me. 'Are you all right?' she asked anxiously.

I could talk now but my breath came hard. 'I'm going to get that bastard,' I muttered.

'What did you say to Novosty?' Heather asked.

'I told him the truth.'

'What happened? Is he the assassin?'

'Novosty told me nothing,' I said. 'He's a very good poker player. But Marsh told me plenty – without saying a word.'

Her lovely blue eyes searched my face.

'Either Novosty has nothing to do with the assassination plot,' I said, 'or Marsh thinks he doesn't, which is possible, of course. It wouldn't be the first time a hired agent was kept in the dark about the real nature of a mission.'

'True.' Heather nodded.

'But somehow I really don't think Novosty has anything to do with the assassination plot.'

'Will he kill us now?' she asked quietly.

There was no point in lying to her.

'Well, even if we are on the wrong trail, it seems that he has to. We know that he's up to something and that it involves the Defence Ministry.'

'I suppose that's what they're doing out there right now,' Heather said, 'plotting our unpleasant demise.'

I moved my wrists against the ropes binding them.

The knot was very tight, too tight to work loose. I looked at the shuttered window. 'They'll probably wait until dark,' I said.

'They wouldn't want to disturb the village,' Heather agreed wryly.

I sat there, twisting the rope binding my wrists and wondering what the hell I could do. Besides Hugo the stiletto, I had Pierre, the cyanide bomb, attached to my thigh and my belt and buckle held plastic explosive and a miniature dart blowgun – all gifts from the imaginative men in Axe's Special Effects and Editing. But Hugo was the only weapon that could free our wrists.

I flexed my right forearm and the stiletto was released from its sheath. But it did not slip into my palm as usual; its route was obstructed by the rope around my wrists. I turned my back to Heather.

'Can you get your hands up to my wrists?' I asked.

She glanced at me and turned her back to mine. 'I don't know. But even if I can, I won't be able to undo the ropes.'

'I know. But look at my right inner wrist. You'll see the tip of a knife there.'

Heather looked and saw. 'Why, Nick, you have the nicest surprises!'

I grinned at her and turned further so she could reach the point of the stiletto. I could feel her working at it. 'Pull it in an even, slow movement,' I said, 'moving it outward and past the ropes.'

She did and in another moment the stiletto slid past

the ropes and clattered to the floor. We glanced anxiously toward the door, but the discussion in the next room continued without interruption.

'Pick up the knife,' I said. Heather bent down and awkwardly retrieved it. 'Grab it firmly by the handle and back up to me again.'

Heather followed orders. 'Cut at the rope,' I said. 'And it would be nice if you got more rope than flesh.'

I felt the blade slide past my palm to the rope and then Heather was slicing at the knot. Finally, after what seemed an eternity, I felt the rope giving. With one last firm stroke Heather cut through. And just in time; the voices in the next room were suddenly still.

I pulled my wrists free and turned quickly to Heather. Taking Hugo, I slashed once at the ropes binding her wrists, severing them. Just then we heard a sound at the door.

'Stay put,' I whispered.

Heather sat on the bed as if she were still bound. I stood up, holding my hands behind me, as the door opened. It was Koval.

'Well,' he said, grinning at us. 'I see you are still here.'

'Are you going to let us go, now that we've told you what we know?' I said. He had left the door partly open and I could see Novosty and Marsh talking together in the next room. Marsh looked eagerly expectant.

'We will see about that,' Koval answered me

blandly. 'For now, we must take you to another place, yes? Where you will be safer.'

He moved past Heather to me. I knew where they were taking us. To some quiet country lane where they would use a silencer or knife. He took my arm. 'Come, we must make a blindfold for both of you. Into the other room, please.'

Heather had gotten up from the bed. I watched her come up behind Koval, clasp her hands together and swing at the back of his neck.

The Russian grunted and fell against me. I held him steady with one hand, smashed my other fist into his face. He yelled and crashed to the floor. I chopped him behind the ear for good measure as he went down. The stiletto was in my belt, but I hadn't had to use it.

'Get his gun!' I told Heather.

I moved up beside the door just as Novosty came running through, his automatic ready. He saw Heather bending over Koval and aimed the gun at her. I brought my hand down hard on his wrist. The gun flew from his grasp and hit the floor, spinning across its polished surface.

I grabbed Novosty's gun hand before the tall Russian could recover and threw him across the room.

Heather was still trying to find Koval's gun. I spotted Novosty's automatic over by the bed and dived for it. I landed beside it and grabbed for the butt. But before I could bring the gun up, Novosty was back on his feet and throwing himself at me. He was a slim, wiry man with plenty of muscle on his lean frame. He hit me hard, trying to wrench the automatic from my grasp. We rolled twice across the floor toward the closed window, Novosty straining for the gun.

I threw a right fist to his head and he hit the floor. Heather had come up with Koval's pistol now, just as Marsh charged into the room. He must have been delayed getting his gun, a Mauser 7.75 Parbellum automatic that looked a lot like Wilhelmina.

His face dark with anger, Marsh rushed into the room, firing and cursing. His shot was intended for Heather, but the aim was bad; the bullet missed her head by six inches. She returned fire, hitting Marsh twice in rapid succession, in the chest and in the neck.

Out of the corner of my eye, I saw Novosty struggle to his feet again and make for the door. Still on the floor, I made a grab for his leg. He kicked out at me viciously. I tried to duck but still the foot connected with the side of my head. I lost my grip on the ankle, and before I could make another grab for him, Novosty was out of the room and heading for the front door.

I looked around quickly. Koval wasn't moving and Marsh lay on his back, groaning, fighting death with every shallow breath.

'Tie him up,' I told Heather, indicating Koval. 'I'm going after Novosty.'

There wasn't time to look for Wilhelmina. Novosty had headed for the black sedan, changed his mind when he realised he didn't have the key and started toward the village main street on the run. By the time I took after him he already had a hundred yards or so on me.

We ran for several blocks and then he disappeared around a corner. When I rounded the corner after him, I saw him starting a small gray Simca whose owner must have left the keys in the ignition. I ran faster, but Novosty pulled away before I could reach the car.

I looked around and got my bearings. Heather had left the keys under the dash of the S.O.C.E.M.A. Gregoire, but where the hell was the thing? I ran to the next corner and looked to my right. Yes, there it was!

I was behind the wheel in a moment and had the key in the ignition, followed by the astonished look of a village woman carrying a string bag of groceries. I turned back out into the main street, as I'd seen Novosty do, shifting up as I went, and saw the Simca several hundred yards ahead of me, heading out of town.

By the time Novosty reached open country, on a winding narrow road, I had closed to a hundred yards and was gaining fast. The shrubbery that lined the road stood well above the height of the cars so whenever Novosty disappeared around a curve, he was out of sight until we hit the straightaway again.

He was skidding crazily around every curve. My sports car was cornering beautifully and soon I was right on him. He had seen me and when I tried to pass him, to force him over, he pulled out to stop me. He managed this on several curves until he met a slow-moving horse-drawn wagon coming from the other direction.

Novosty wheeled the Simca to the right. It skidded and came back to the left, catching the back corner of the wagon which was loaded with bales of hay. The wagon tipped toward the ditch, then swayed back and tipped part of its contents into the road in front of me. I drove on through it with hay scattering in all directions and my view momentarily obscured.

When I came out of the hay cloud I was right on top of the Simca. I tried to come up alongside but Novosty pulled over in front of me. I yanked my wheel hard right and Novosty followed, as I thought he would, then I pulled hard to the left and shifted down. The S.O.C.E.M.A.-Gregoire leaped ahead as my foot went down on the accelerator and moved up beside the Simca before Novosty could pull back over.

Novosty jerked hard on the wheel, crashed the Simca into the right side of the sports car, the driver's side. I retaliated by slamming the sports car back against the Simca, edging Novosty toward the edge of the road. He almost lost control but recovered quickly, jumped momentarily ahead of me.

We tore around another curve, oblivious to what might be coming from the other direction. I pulled even with Novosty again, but before I could make my move, he slammed his Simca into my side.

Now it was my turn to lose control. The wheel jerked from my grasp and in the next instant the sports car rocketed off the road into a large open meadow. I saw Novosty's car careering crazily toward the opposite side and a twenty-foot drop-off to a rocky field, then I was hurtling through the air, the car beginning a roll before it hit.

I saw a flash of sky and then of brown earth. There was a jarring crash and the door on my side popped open and I was thrown out. I hit the ground, rolled twice and lay there stunned. The car kept on rolling and ended up, against a towering boulder.

I sat up slowly, moving gingerly. I ached, but there appeared to be no broken bones. Then I heard the explosion from across the road. I struggled to my feet. I had to save Novosty – if he could still be saved.

I stumbled up to the road and saw the Russian had gone over. Black smoke was spiraling up from below. I moved to the edge of the drop and looked down. The Simca was wrapped in flame. I could see Novosty, unconscious or dead, inside. I was too late; I couldn't possibly get to him.

I stood there watching the Simca burn and couldn't help wondering when my day would come and some Russian or Chicom agent would witness my death. No agent lived forever; most didn't even make it to old age. That was why Hawk always said when we parted, 'So long, Nick. Good luck. I'll see you when I see you.' Which might be never.

I heard a car engine and turned just as a small white Lancia pulled over a few yards behind me. Heather jumped out and ran over to me. A bewildered Englishman crawled out of the other door of the car and stood staring wide-eyed at the burning Simca.

'Oh dear,' Heather said, looking down at the flaming wreck. Then she turned and looked across to where the S.O.C.E.M.A. lay upsidedown in the field on the other side of the road. It was a mess.

'Sorry about that,' I said.

'Oh, well,' she sighed. 'It never shifted down very well, anyway.'

I grinned at her. 'That Ferodo clutch must have needed adjusting.'

'Rather. Are you hurt?'

'Just my ego. I wanted Novosty alive. Now he can't tell us anything.'

She gave me a small, smug smile. 'Marsh talked before he died. I promised him a doctor, poor chap. It seems these lads had nothing to do with the assassination. They planned to steal guided missile blueprints as they were transferred from the Defence Ministry to military headquarters.'

'I'll be damned,' I said. So, I had been right about Novosty all along. But if the Russians weren't behind the assassination plot then who was?

Six

Brutus was seated behind his desk, fingering the photograph of Fergus' commando unit. In front of him was a stack full of official Army records, each containing information on the men in the unit.

'We've managed to track all of them down,' Brutus said. 'Twelve of them are dead, either killed in the war or died at home. This one,' he pointed at a man wearing a lieutenant's insignia, 'is a very interesting one. Lieutenant John Elmore. He had part of his skull crushed in a commando raid. Had a steel plate put in his head. After he left the service, he put his commando training to work for him. He became the most successful paid assassin in England. Mostly underworld assignments. The man was a genius at killing.'

I arched my eyebrows. Here, at last, was something.

Brutus shot my hopes down immediately. 'He was killed years ago in a fight with Scotland Yard in a suburb of London.'

'Are you sure it was him?'

'Certain! Scotland Yard got a tip from one of its informers that Elmore was hiding in a service station. When they got there, he started shooting. One of the Yard men got a good look at him through the telescopic sights of a sniper's rifle. The fight lasted 10 minutes, then the whole place went up in flames. One of the bullets must have hit a petrol pump. When it was all over they found Elmore's body burned to a crisp. But there is no doubt that it was him.'

'So that leaves us with a killer still running loose.'

Brutus didn't think so. 'It's twenty-four hours past the fortnight deadline,' Brutus was saying, walking back and forth before his massive desk, pulling on a heavy briar pipe clenched tightly between his teeth. 'Which could mean your man Marsh was deliberately misled by Novosty so as not to give away the real purpose of the mission. In that case, my lad, the assassin died in that flaming car. And with the others dead or in custody, the plot has been frustrated.'

'But Koval has verified Marsh's story,' Heather pointed out.

'But wouldn't he do just that?' Brutus argued. 'If you were Koval, would you rather be tried for stealing some documents or for murder?'

'A good point,' I said. 'I can't help thinking, though, that our killer is still out there somewhere.'

'The handwriting is bothering you, isn't it?' Brutus said, sucking at his pipe.

'Yes, sir. And the way the killings were done. When you've been at this work for a while, you get a feeling about a man you're after, whether you've ever met him or not. My idea of the killer just doesn't match up with Novosty.'

'Well, I hope you're wrong, Nick,' Brutus said heavily. 'Because if you're right, all we can do at this point is double our guard on all our high officials and wait.'

'I know,' I said gloomily.

Brutus suddenly stuck his big jaw out and grinned. 'All right, my lad. Don't look so down. You and Heather here go on about your work and check with me often.'

'We're off, then,' Heather said. 'We'll divide up the work. I'll take the Home Secretary and the Lord Privy Seal and Nick can start off with the Foreign Secretary. We'll give you a ring tonight, Brutus.'

I walked down the wide corridor slowly. At first glance, the office building seemed to be humming in the ordinary way of a day's work, the secretaries hurrying from one room to another, typewriters clacking behind closed doors. But if you knew what to look for, you saw the undercurrent of tension beneath the surface.

Those same secretaries avoided dark corridors and unused rooms. There were government agents and plain-clothes Yard men everywhere. They stopped me every couple of minutes and made me flash the I.D. Brutus had given me. I wondered how difficult it might be to forge an SOE or MI5 I.D. card, probably not too hard for a knowledgeable operator.

I climbed the stairs to the next floor and headed toward the Foreign Secretary's offices. There were a lot of people in the corridor here, including a small contingent of uniformed soldiers at the wide doors leading to the main work areas.

Across the corridor was a smaller unguarded door to a suite of lesser offices of the Ministry. As I moved past this, a man came out. He was wearing a janitor's uniform and carrying a mop and bucket, and he seemed to be in a great hurry – he almost knocked me down.

He gave me a quick, hard look and then he was moving quickly down the corridor, almost running. He was a tall man with dark hair and a mustache. I was trying to decide whether or not the mustache was phony, about to take off after him, when I heard the scream.

It came from the offices the janitor had just left. A man in a dark suit and tie got in my way. I shoved him aside and opened the door.

As I moved into the office, leaving the door wide open behind me, a girl standing near the doorway leading to the next room looked at me wide-eyed and screamed. Papers she must have been holding lay scattered at her feet. I moved past her into a small private office as footsteps pounded down the corridor behind me. Inside the inner office, a dark-haired woman stood over the body of the Foreign Secretary, her mouth opening and closing in shock.

I saw the horror in her face and looked at the reason for it. The Secretary had been killed with a garrotte, the kind used by the commandos in the war. He had been almost decapitated and blood was spattered everywhere.

The woman looked at me and tried to speak but I moved her to a chair and sat her in it, then I looked around the room. There was a note propped on a desk nearby, but I ignored it for the moment.

I thought about looking for that janitor but decided against it. He'd be long gone by now. I tried to fix in my mind how he'd looked, what had made me think the mustache might be phony, and that's when I remembered something. Not just the mustache but the hair must have been phony – a wig – because I was sure I'd seen a fringe of blond hair at the back of the neck.

Two men stormed into the office now.

'Here, what's going on here?' one asked.

'Bloody hell!' the other said, spotting the dead man.

'And who are you?' The first man looked at me suspiciously.

I flashed my I.D. card as more people came running into the room. 'I think I got a look at the killer,' I said.

'He's dressed like a janitor. Ran that way down the corridor.'

One of the men hurried from the room. The others eyed me warily, as the room filled with horrified Ministry personnel. I went to the desk and looked at the note. It read:

'Better late than never. The amount owed and payable has now risen to fourteen million pounds. Put it aboard a private plane and fly it to Geneva. You will receive further instructions as to what bank to contact for deposit. Don't fail – you're running out of time.'

'Here, what have you got there?' a plainclothes policeman said beside me. 'I'll just take that.' He reached for the note stiffly and I let him have it. It had looked like the same handwriting to me but of course the handwriting expert would have to confirm it.

I moved from the desk to get another look at the body. There were reporters in the outer room now, trying unsuccessfully to get past the military guards there.

As I walked around the desk closer to the body, I spotted a scrap of paper on the floor just about where the killer might have been standing when he took the note out of his pocket and placed it on the desk. I picked it up; it appeared to be torn from a piece of stationery, just a corner of the sheet. There was a phone number written on it, in pencil. A part of a printed emblem remained on the tear-line.

Studying the scrawled digits, it seemed to me that they might have been written by the same hand that wrote the assassination notes. It was a long shot, certainly, but we needed one right now.

A burly man moved toward me and I slipped the paper into my pocket.

'You there – who are you?'

'SOE,' I said, showing the I.D. again. He hadn't seen me hide the paper.

'Oh. Right. Just keep out of the way, my lad.'

'I'll make every effort to,' I said, straight-faced. I moved over to the body for a last look at the mess that had been the Secretary.

It was another unnecessarily bloody killing. The garrotte, composed in this case of two metal handles with a length of piano wire running between them, was a familiar weapon to military men. The attacker merely looped the wire over the victim's head and pulled. The wire cut through flesh, muscle, tendon and bone until it separated head from body. At least it was a fast way to go. I remembered, suddenly, that Augie Fergus had served in the commandos. Was that how he came to know the assassin? If, in fact, he *had* known him. Now I was playing a guessing game and there was no time for that. I turned and quickly left the room.

I found Heather at the Home Secretary's office nearby; she hadn't heard about the latest slaying. 'I just ran into Elmo Jupiter,' she said lightly. 'He insisted that I call him. Are you jealous, love?'

'I wish I had the time,' I said. 'The Foreign Secretary has just been assassinated.'

Her lovely blue eyes widened in shock.

'Does Brutus know?' she asked.

'I called him on the way here. He was in quite a state.'

'It's bloody awful, isn't it?' she said.

'If we don't improve on our batting average soon,' I told her, 'the British government will cease to exist as a viable institution. There was total panic at the Ministry.'

'Does Brutus have any ideas?' she asked.

'Not really. We're pretty much on our own now. The Prime Minister has already been notified, I hear, and wants to deliver the ransom immediately.'

'He is probably afraid he may be next.'

'He's a logical target,' I said. 'The killer left another note, demanding payment. And I found this at the scene.' I handed her the scrap of paper.

'It's the telephone number of the Ministry,' she said, puzzled. 'Do you think the assassin wrote it?'

'It seems unlikely that an employee at the Ministry would need to write the number down,' I said. 'And the scrawl seems similar to the handwriting in the assassination notes. What do you make of the emblem?'

'There isn't quite enough of it showing,' she said. 'But somehow I think I've seen it before. Let's go up to my flat and have a closer look.'

Heather leased a small apartment in London's West End. It was a three-flight walk up but once inside it was quite a charming place. She made us a cup of

English tea and we sat at a small table by the window sipping it. I pulled the scrap of paper from my pocket again.

'Whoever this fellow is, he likes to play rough,' I said, turning the paper over in my hand. I had given Heather the details of the killing. 'Rougher than Novosty. And he's probably more dangerous because he enjoys killing and because he's probably not rational.'

I held the paper to the light from the window. 'Hey, what's this ? There's the impression of some writing on here, under the digits.'

Heather got up and looked over my shoulder. 'What does it say, Nick ?'

'I can't make it out. It looks like a capital "R" to start, and then – '

'An "O" and a "Y", ' Heather said excitedly.

'And then – "A" and maybe "L". Royal. And there's something else.'

'It might be "Ho",' she said, 'and part of a "T". There is a Royal Hotel, you know, at Russell Square.'

'Of course,' I said. 'Royal Hotel. But is this hotel stationery ?'

'I don't think so,' Heather said. 'I told you that I've seen that emblem before, but I don't associate it with a hotel. We'll check it out though.'

'If it isn't hotel paper,' I said, 'we have a double clue. Royal Hotel and the organisation or idea represented by the symbol.'

'Exactly,' Heather agreed, excitement showing in her face. 'Maybe this is our break, Nick.'

'*If* the paper belonged to the killer,' I reminded her.

After tea we took a taxi to the Royal Hotel and spoke to the assistant manager at the desk. He looked at the scrap of paper and denied that it belong to the hotel. He took out a sheet of hotel stationery and showed it to us for comparison.

'Of course, it might have belonged to a guest,' the man said. 'Or to one of the many conventioneers who meet here.'

'Yes,' I said heavily. 'Well, thanks just the same.'

Outside, Heather said, 'I think we'd better bring Brutus up to date.'

'All right,' I said. 'Maybe he can offer some ideas on our emblem.' We hailed a cab and went directly to Brutus's office.

When we got there, after marching briskly through the long corridor with the uniformed security guards, we found Brutus poring over old police records. He thought there might still be some chance that the assassin was a convicted felon with a grudge against the Establishment. I showed him the scrap of paper, but he shook his head.

'I can't make anything of it,' he said. 'I can make copies though and show it around the department. Maybe somebody will recognise it.'

'That might be worthwhile, sir,' I said.

'We've checked out this janitor chap you saw leaving the Secretary's office,' Brutus told me. 'Nobody can identify a person of that description working in the building.'

'That figures,' I said.

'He's probably our killer,' Heather said. 'You were close enough to grab him, Nick.'

'Don't remind me,' I said glumly.

'Don't blame yourself, lad,' Brutus said, lighting his pipe. 'If it weren't for you, we'd have nothing.'

'We may still have nothing,' I said. 'If it's of any use to you, I have a hazy memory of seeing blond hair under the dark, as if the man might have been wearing a wig.'

Brutus made a note on a slip of paper. 'Probably the mustache was false too.'

'Probably. I know I thought so when I saw it.'

Brutus rose from his desk and moved around it, sucking at his pipe. He looked very tired, as if he hadn't slept in days.

'At the moment,' he said, 'despite the clues, we're a long way from solving the assassination plot. The third note found at the scene tells us nothing more about our man. Or men.'

'If the assassin had accomplices,' Heather said, 'he seems to make sparing use of them.'

'Yes, the killings certainly appear to have been accomplished by the same man – although they could give that appearance if directed by one man. At any rate, the Prime Minister has confided to me that he is arranging for payment of the sum demanded.'

'Fourteen million *pounds*?' Heather asked.

'Precisely. We discussed the possibility of tricking our man somehow, loading the plane with phoney money or the like. But there seems little opportunity, the way he has it worked out. The PM will be going to the banks tomorrow for the funds.'

I stroked my chin. 'I wonder, sir, if money is what this man really wants.'

'What do you mean?' Brutus asked.

'He may think he wants the money, on a conscious level,' I said, slowly, 'but on another level – a more primitive one, a darker one – he may only want to kill.'

Brutus sucked his pipe and studied my face. 'Yes, I get your meaning. But be that as it may, we must assume that payment of the sum demanded will stop the killings, mustn't we?'

'Yes, sir, I suppose so,' I said.

'Right. Well, you two can get some rest now. Keep after that scrap of paper though – there might be something there.'

Heather rose from her usual perch on Brutus's desk and I got up from my chair.

'There's one other thing, sir,' I said.

'Yes?'

'Hawk told me Augie Fergus had served in the commandos. I think we should get a list of the men in Augie's outfit.'

Brutus frowned. 'That could be quite a list.'

'I'd restrict it to the men in his immediate company. There might be a lead in it.'

'Right, Nick,' Brutus said. 'I'll get on it. Anything else?'

'Just a few hours sleep,' I said, grinning.

'I promise not to bother either of you for the rest of the day,' he said. 'Get yourselves a good meal and some rest.'

'Thanks,' I said.

Heather and I had dinner at a quiet little restaurant, and then she invited me to her flat for a drink before I returned to my SOE-paid hotel room. I had a bourbon and she took sherry. We sat on a long sofa sipping the drinks.

'I wish I could remember where I've seen the emblem on that scrap of paper,' she confessed. 'I know I've seen it somewhere and not too long ago.'

'There's plenty of time for that tomorrow when you're rested,' I said. 'Let it all incubate inside until then.'

'All right, doctor.' She smiled. 'I put myself completely under your care.'

'Is that a proposition?'

'Take it as you like.'

I put my unfinished drink down and reached for her. She melted into my arms, her softness pressing into me. She was wearing a pants suit and shirt and no bra. As I pressed my lips to hers, I brushed my hand across her right breast. The nipple hardened at my touch. My tongue explored her mouth and she responded passionately.

She broke away from me and stood up. 'I'll get into

something more – appropriate,' she said.

She disappeared into the bedroom and I finished my bourbon. The warmth of the liquor spread all through me. I was relaxed and ready. And then Heather returned.

She was wearing an almost-transparent floor-length peignoir.

I undressed and lay down beside her on the sofa. I slid my hand between her thighs and caressed her. A soft sound purred in her throat.

I slipped the peignoir over her head and let it fall to the floor beside me. And she wanted me. It was clear that she wanted me very much. I knew that this would be even better than the last time.

We began leisurely, comfortably, letting the ripples of pleasure pass through us as our bodies touched and the fire slowly flamed up inside. It was sweet, very sweet; the leisurely pace stoked the fire and built it.

As the thrusting and reaching and probing reached a greater intensity, Heather began to tremble. The sounds in her throat grew until they seemed to fill the room. Then it was a primitive plunging, savage in its intensity, as Heather's arms locked tightly around me, her hot thighs pressing me into her, deeper and deeper.

When it was over, I lay back, lit a cigarette and thought about Heather and Hadiya; I couldn't help comparing the two of them. Their ways of making love were as different as their nationalities. Hadiya's was like the North African desert in which she was born: fevered, like a raging sand storm which ended as abruptly as it began. Heather's was more like the English spring: slow to develop, following a long-established pattern, gradually easing into the heat of summer, then tapering off into the cooling spell of fall.

Which was better? I couldn't tell. Each had its advantages. But it would be nice, I thought, to have a steady diet of first one, then the other.

Seven

It was after midnight when I got back to my hotel room and to bed to sleep. About an hour after I dozed off, I awoke suddenly. At first I had no idea what had awakened me and then I heard if again: a soft clicking sound. What was it? And was it inside the room or out?

I lay listening, wanting very much to go back to sleep and knowing that that was a luxury I could not afford. Many an agent has awakened dead, so to speak, because he was too tired or sleepy to check out a strange noise in the middle of the night.

I lay perfectly still, staring into the blackness.

Silence surrounded me, punctuated by the traffic noise from the street outside. Was I imagining things, or dreaming?

Fifteen minutes by the luminous face of my watch. I yawned and struggled to keep my eyes open. A half-hour. Surely I had been mistaken. Sleep was pulling at me, dragging me down into its dark, warm pit. My eyelids closed, then popped wide open.

That sound again! That small clicking sound and this time there was no doubt. It came from the door to the corridor. Somebody was moving a key in the lock.

The sound was repeated. Whoever was out there was satisfied that I was asleep.

I eased silently out of bed. The only light in the room came from the window and under the door to the corridor. Now a shadow blocked out the narrow ribbon of light under the door. Yes, somebody was outside and coming in shortly.

I pulled on my pants and a shirt, slipped into my shoes as the tumbler clicked in the lock and the knob began turning. I moved to the chair where my jacket was hanging and reached for the shoulder holster under it. I pulled Wilhelmina free then moved back to the bed and drew the sheet up over the pillow. When the door eased open, I was crouched behind the chair.

A thick-shouldered man entered the room slowly, holding a hand gun in front of him. Another thinner man moved shadow-like behind him. They came into the room soundlessly and stood facing the bed. The thick-shouldered man nodded to the slim one and they aimed their guns at the bed where I had been lying. It was hidden in shadow and they thought I was still there. The guns, big and ugly, had long silencers fitted to their muzzles. Suddenly, three or four shots popped from each gun. I waited until they stopped firing and the bedding was a riddled mess, then I reached up and switched on the light.

'Surprise!' I said, holding Wilhelmina on them.

They whirled to face me, confusion on their faces. I had never seen either of them before.

'Drop the guns,' I said firmly.

Apparently I wasn't very persuasive. The thick-shouldered one moved his gun and fired quickly, dropping to one knee. His shot chipped wood from the frame of the overstuffed chair I was using for cover. I ducked as he fired a second time. This time the slug slammed into the chair stuffing.

I hit the floor behind the chair, rolled once and came up firing on the far side. Wilhelmina, sans silencer, roared loudly in the room, the slug tearing into the wall behind the brawny gunman's head. I fired again quickly and the second shot caught the man in the chest, grand-slammed him against the wall. He slid to the floor, leaving a crimson mark on the wall.

The second gunman now popped off another round, chipping flowered paper off the wall behind me, and dived for cover behind the bed. I snapped off a crashing shot but missed my target by inches and shattered the leg of a night table.

I was back behind the chair now. I picked up a

fallen ashtray, heaved it to my right and drew fire from my enemy. In the same instant, I moved back to my left, grabbed above my head at the light switch again, darkening the room. I scrambled quickly to the side of a large chest of drawers which afforded good cover from the bed.

The surviving gunman was on his feet, moving toward the door from the bed, firing toward me as he went. The slugs chewed up the wood on the front of the chest. I stayed down, but as he headed out the door I managed to fire another round at him. Unfortunately I missed.

I jumped to my feet and sprang for the door, just in time to see the gunman disappear around the corner in the corridor. He was heading for the back stairs.

I swore under my breath as I stepped quickly back into the room. I grabbed a small attache case and took out a spare magazine for Wilhelmina. I thumbed the old magazine out and then jammed in the new. Then I raced out into the corridor, past a small gathering of wide-eyed hotel personnel and guests, to the back stairs.

By the time I reached the bottom of the stairs and moved out into the alley behind the hotel, the second gunman was nowhere in sight. I ran to the mouth of the alley, looked right then left – and spotted him just turning a corner. I started after him.

I was gaining on him when we emerged into High Holborn, at Euston Square and he saw the entrance to the Tube – the London subway – and dived into it.

I was there in a moment. As I reached the stairs, I saw him at the bottom, aiming his gun at me. He pulled the trigger but the only sound was a futile click. Apparently the gun had misfired. He swore and threw it down.

'Hold it!' I yelled.

But he disappeared around the bottom of the stairs. I stuck the Luger into my belt and followed.

We hurdled barriers and then I was racing after him along the station platform. An elderly man standing at the edge of the platform, waiting for a train gaped at us as we raced by.

At the end of the platform my man started climbing stairs to another level. He turned and I got a good look at him. He was young and tough; there was both anger and desperation in his face. He bolted up the steps with me close behind.

At the top of the stairs he turned and waited for me. As I closed the distance he kicked out viciously. I fell back a couple of steps and almost lost my balance completely. By the time I reached the top of the stairs, the gunman was already halfway down the platform. I ran after him, trying to regain the ground I had lost.

A train roared into the station but my man made no attempt to board it. Apparently he felt he had a better chance in the station. At the end of the platform, he plummeted down into another stairwell.

A train was just pulling away here. A middle-aged couple had gotten off and seated themselves on a bench. They looked up placidly as the gunman, after a glance back at me, began running again down the platform. But I caught up with him just past the bench. I made a diving lunge and brought him down.

We fell heavily, rolling at the feet of the couple on the bench. They sat there, watching with mild interest, as the man grabbed for my throat.

I broke free with a chop to his forearm, then delivered another chop to his neck. He fell backward. I struggled up on one knee and punched a fist into his face.

He grunted under the impact, but he was not finished. He kicked out at me as I threw myself at him, the blow knocking me sidewise to the edge of the platform. I almost went over.

He saw how close I was to the edge and decided to give me a little help. He kicked, aiming for my side, just as a train came into the station. I grabbed his foot and held on. He tried to jerk free, lost his balance and cartwheeled off the edge of the platform, nearly dragging me with him. His scream was drowned by the train as it roared over him.

The couple who had watched us so placidly were on their feet now, the woman shrieking like a stuck factory whistle.

I turned and headed quickly up the steps. I did not want to explain all this to the police. Not just at the moment.

Eight

'I've got it!' Heather said as I let her into my room. 'I've remembered about that emblem!'

I rubbed sleep out of my eyes and followed her inside. She stopped short and stared. Thanks to my uninvited visitors, the place looked like a disaster area.

'What in the world happened here?'

'You'd never believe it.'

'Try me,' she said.

'A good guess is that the assassin knows I'm on the case and has decided he doesn't want me breathing down his neck. He sent a couple of big fellows with big guns to deliver a one-way ticket to the morgue. I had to get Brutus to pull the police off my back at three A.M.'

'But how would the assassin know who you are and what you're here for?' she asked, puzzled.

I shrugged. 'A leak in Brutus's office?' I suggested. 'Impossible!' She was indignant.

'I hope so,' I said. 'Anyway, it means we're getting warm so – what about that emblem?'

Her face brightened again excitedly. 'Let me see that paper.'

I handed it to her. 'Yes,' she nodded, 'I'm sure of it. It's part of a design for an auto emblem. I just can't remember which one.'

I pulled on a shirt and buttoned it. I was beginning to get excited too. 'Let's go back and talk to that fellow at the Royal Hotel again,' I said. 'That may just be faster than trying to get a list of emblems from the AA.'

'I have a taxi waiting.'

We drove through a dissipating fog along Millbank, past the massive edifices of Westminster Abbey and the Houses of Parliament. I knew the House of Commons was in an emergency session at that very moment, debating how to best implement the Prime Minister's decision to comply with the assassin's demand for a fortune in sterling.

At the Royal Hotel, Heather told our man, 'We think we may have identified the symbol on the paper we showed you. It seems to me that I've seen it in connection with an automobile.'

108

The hotel clerk thought a moment. 'You may be right,' he said, finally.

'Have you had any guests recently who might have been in London representing some auto firm?' I asked.

He gave us a big smile. 'Not a fortnight ago we had a convention of auto makers here.'

'Really?' Heather said.

'Quite!' The man was getting as excited as we were. 'I can give you a list of all the firms that were represented. In fact, I believe we still have some of the literature they passed around in back, waiting for pickup. Would you like to take a look?'

'Yes we would. Thanks,' I said.

He took us to a small storeroom at the rear of the main floor. There were boxes of pamphlets and note paper stacked in a corner. A couple of boxes bore insignia but none that seemed to fit ours.

The desk man went back to his work and we were alone. Heather started looking through one cardboard carton and I took another. Suddenly Heather gave a sharp cry of recognition.

'We've got it, Nick! Look!' She was holding a sheet of paper the same manila color as ours. I moved over to her and studied it.

'Well,' I said. 'Well, well, well.'

The complete emblem showed a scorpion on a field of vine leaves set on a crest shield. We looked at the name of the company printed in an arc above the shield, then at each other.

'Jupiter Motors Limited,' Heather said, her face suddenly changing. 'Yes, of course.'

'Jupiter,' I said. 'Isn't that your friend?'

'Elmo Jupiter isn't my friend,' Heather said flatly. 'But he does own Jupiter Motors. Now I know why the emblem seemed familiar. I've been to one of his showrooms. His plant and offices are on the outskirts of London somewhere.'

'Interesting,' I said. Something about Elmo Jupiter was tugging at the edge of my mind but I couldn't bring it into focus. I stuck the sheet of note paper, along with the original scrap, into my pocket and steered Heather out of the storeroom and back to the desk.

The hotel clerk was delighted when we told him that we had matched the emblem.

'Smashing!' he said.

'Yes,' I agreed. 'Now maybe you can do us one more good turn.'

'Pleased to.'

'We'd like a list of the Jupiter Motors personnel who attended the meetings, if you can manage it.'

'Certainly! We were given a list for each company by the organiser of the affair. I'm sure I still have it somewhere. Excuse me a moment.'

He was back shortly with the list and showed us the names of the Jupiter Motors people. There were three: Derek Forsythe, Percival Smythe and Elmo Jupiter himself.

I thanked the clerk for all his help and Heather and

I walked toward the park at Russell Square, slowly, to let our new-found information sink in.

'Jupiter is a Scorpio,' Heather said. 'Astrologically, I mean. I remember his telling me. That's why the emblem features the scorpion.'

'I think, Heather, we should go see Mr Jupiter,' I said.

Jupiter Motors was in a modern building complex out on North End Road. A lot of money had obviously been put into the place. Still, it showed signs of neglect. After a brief exchange with Jupiter's private secretary, we went into his office. He was all smiles, ignoring me and concentrating on Heather.

'Well, Heather!' he said warmly. 'What a pleasant surprise.'

'You told me to get in touch,' Heather said as he took her hand and held it. 'Richard here is frightfully interested in cars and hoped he could have a look through your plant.'

Jupiter focused his hard brown eyes on me. He wasn't bad-looking, I had to admit, with an athletic, muscular build. But those hard eyes spoiled an otherwise handsome face.

'Of course you may look around.' He gave me a tight smile. 'It will give me a chance to chat with Heather.'

Heather gave him a warm look. I watched his face. He seemed to be studying her now, as if trying to determine if she were friend or enemy.

He pushed the intercom button and asked his secretary to call a Mr Burroughs who would show me around while Jupiter and Heather had tea in a lounge down the corridor.

As we waited for Mr Burroughs, I said to Jupiter casually, 'I understand there was an auto manufacturers' convention here in London recently.'

'Yes.' He nodded. 'I attended with my sales director and his assistant. The meetings fell far short of expectations. There's too little cooperation between companies here in England.'

'It's the same in the States, I think,' I said.

'Yes,' he said slowly. 'And what is it you do there, Mr Matthews?'

'I'm in public health, same as Heather here. She's been assigned to show me London.'

Heather pulled out a cigarette and deliberately fumbled her lighter. It fell to the carpeted floor. I stood as if to pick the thing up for her but Jupiter beat me to it. As he lighted her cigarette, I pressed the stem on the watch I was wearing. Besides keeping perfect time it took excellent pictures.

The intercom buzzed. Jupiter reached over and flicked the switch. 'Yes? Good, send him right in.' He glanced over at me. 'It's Burroughs at last.'

Mr Burroughs was amiable but almost as bored as I was with the tour. In the sales division I was introduced to Forsythe and Smythe, the two men who'd attended the convention at the Royal Hotel with Jupiter. Forsythe was a gray-haired distinguished type; Smythe about fifteen years his junior and pushy, the type of salesman who shoves his foot in the door when he's selling house to house. Somehow I didn't see either of them as our man, but we'd have Brutus check them out anyway.

Jupiter seemed a bit tense when Heather and I said good-bye finally. He focused those cold eyes on me and said, with complete insincerity, 'Come back any time, Mr Matthews. Glad to have you.'

'Thanks,' I said, returning the chilly stare.

Walking toward West Kensington station, Heather and I assessed our morning's work. 'Burroughs hinted the company is in financial trouble because of high government taxes,' I told her.

'Interesting,' she said. 'I got a set of prints, I think, on the cigarette lighter. Did you manage any photos?'

'One of him and a couple of the papers on his desk, for his handwriting.' I lit cigarettes for us as we walked. 'I also met Forsythe and Smythe, but I think Jupiter is our man. I'd just like to know how he found out I'm an agent.'

'He knows I'm an agent too,' Heather said. 'I'm sure of it. But we got what we wanted and that's the important thing.'

'I just hope it all adds up to something,' I said.

She regarded me soberly. 'I remembered something else, Nick, while I had tea with Jupiter. Remember the day the Foreign Secretary was assassinated, I told you I'd run into Elmo Jupiter when I met you outside?'

I stopped and looked at her. I had forgotten that.

'Yes,' I said slowly, something stirring in my memory, 'you said you'd just seen him, right near the Foreign Office. What was he doing around there, did he say?'

She shook her head. 'Not really. Oh, I went through the usual polite bit, "Why, Elmo Jupiter, what brings you to this part of town?" I think he said a friend but I wasn't really listening. Then he started pressing for a date and I got away as soon as I decently could.'

' "A friend",' I said, shaking my head. 'It's always possible, of course, but it's too much of a coincidence.'

'I certainly could believe he's our killer' Heather said shuddering. 'Those eyes! They give me the creeps.'

I stopped dead. 'That's it! The janitor! That's what's been working at the back of my mind. He had the same build as Jupiter and the same hard-looking eyes. I was right – the hair and mustache were phony. It *was* Jupiter I'm sure of it. And it fits! He recognised me when he bumped into me in the corridor and concluded rightly, that I was with the security people. He was afraid of just this, afraid I'd see him again and remember, so he sent those thugs to kill me.'

'I think it's time for another chat with Brutus,' Heather said.

We found her boss in his office. He was in a foul mood, having just returned from London Airport where he had been overseeing the loading of fourteen million pounds sterling aboard a military jet. The money had been packed in steel boxes and guarded by SOE agents.

We briefed him on our trip to Jupiter Motors, then gave Brutus Heather's cigarette lighter and the film from my watch camera. He rushed them to scientific division and we settled down to wait.

The results were not long in coming, only a half hour. A clerk handed Brutus a folded file. As he read it, his brow furrowed. Finally he said, 'It seems, Nick, you and Heather have gotten the fingerprints of a dead man.'

He handed me the file. The first page was the police record of John Elmore.

'There's no doubt?' I asked.

Brutus shook his head gravely. 'The fingerprints match perfectly.'

'Then he must have staged that fight with Scotland Yard, left a body behind and sneaked out somehow while the fire was raging. He could have had plastic surgery performed on his face and gone into the automobile business. All these years he was operating in the clear. But why now, out of the blue, would he . . .'

'We'll find out after we pick him up,' Brutus said, reaching for the telephone.

'You'd better pick good men, sir,' I told him. 'If Jupiter is our man, and it certainly looks like it, he's very clever. And extremely dangerous.'

'No need to remind me,' Brutus huffed.

After he got off the phone I offered to go along with

his men. 'No need,' he brushed off my offer. 'You two've done enough today.'

'What about the money now?' Heather asked him.

'I've spoken to the Prime Minister – the white flag is flying above Parliament and he is not impressed yet with what we've done so far. He remembers Novosty.'

'But this is different!' Heather pleaded.

'You have to remember,' Brutus said, 'that absolute panic reigns at the moment. Parliament insists that something be done to stop the killings. And the shipment can still be stopped in Switzerland if Elmo Jupiter does turn out to be the assassin.'

We left him a few moments later and walked through the building, headed for the parking area and the beautiful yellow Porsche 911 Heather had rented.

'I think we're entitled to a good lunch,' she said as we reached the car.

I agreed. 'I'm famished.'

Heather started to get behind the wheel, but I stopped her. 'You're not the only sports car buff in the crowd.'

I took the wheel. She chuckled and climbed in beside me. 'Do you like Greek mousaka?' she asked.

'If it's made with plenty of meat,' I said, starting the engine.

'Then I'll make you a nice meal while we wait to hear from Brutus,' she said.

We were lying side by side on the long sofa in

Heather's flat. I was digesting the mousaka, which had been delicious. Heather was certainly an amazing girl.

'A penny for your thoughts,' she said. She was lying against my chest, running a hand seductively along my jaw.

I took the hint and turned to her. I buried my face in her hair, drawing in the scent of her perfume. I nibbled on her ear and she uttered a low, deep moan. She lifted her face to mine, and as I kissed her I undid the row of buttons of her housecoat. I slipped around her back, found the clasp of her bra and unsnapped it. She pulled the housecoat off her shoulders and threw the bra away. I played with her nipples, teasing them with my teeth. They grew hard as pebbles.

Slowly I caressed her shoulder, then the outer rim of her breast. She sucked in her breath sharply when I did that, then bit down on my lip.

Lightly I ran my fingers over her thighs and hips, distributed kisses across her breast. That was as much as she could take.

She guided me to her, making the union herself, arching her lovely back into it and thrusting to meet me until I was deep in her. The familiar sound of pleasure purred in her throat. My mind and body centered on the primal urge to penetrate and explore and ravish this lovely female who was, for the moment, part of me. Our passion grew, mounted . . . and erupted in total fulfillment.

Nine

The phone rang just minutes after we'd finished. Heather put the receiver to her ear, listened a few moments, then gasped. 'Yes sir, right away,' she said, then hung up.

'Brutus?' I asked.

'Yes,' her head bobbed up and down. 'Jupiter has disappeared. He's nowhere to be found, not at his office or his home.'

'Maybe he is just out.'

'Brutus doesn't think so,' she said. 'He believes Jupiter suspects we know about him.'

I pondered that for a second. Brutus was probably right. A man with Jupiter's intelligence would suspect something about our sudden visit to his place. After thinking about it he'd probably decided to play it safe, to hide out somewhere.

I got off the sofa and started to dress. Heather headed for the bedroom. 'Brutus wants to see us immediately, if not sooner, at his office,' she said over her shoulder.

We were ready in ten minutes and walked down the stairs from Heather's flat to the street. It was late afternoon and the early autumn sun was already setting. The sleek Porsche 911 was parked around the corner on a cobblestoned side street. Just as we reached the car, two men stepped out of a building entrance and confronted us. Each held a revolver in his right hand.

'Blimey!' Heather said softly.

'Hold it just there,' the man closest to us said. He was a narrow-shouldered, thin-faced character whose pale blue eyes never left my face. His buddy was stockier with a soccer player's legs. 'Search the girl,' the thin man told him, then, to me, 'Stand still.'

He patted me down and he did a good job – he found Wilhelmina and Hugo.

'What's all this?' I asked, though I could make a good guess.

'Never mind,' the soccer player said, shoving Heather's little purse with the Sterling in his pocket. He nodded toward the curb where a black Rolls-

Royce was pulling up in front of the Porsche. 'Just hop in.'

We didn't seem to have much choice. Heather went first, the thin man moving up beside her. I followed with his pal.

'Where are you taking us?' Heather asked.

'You'll find out,' the thin man said. We were at the curb now. 'Get in.'

'And no funny business,' the man beside me added.

The driver of the Rolls made no move to get out of the car. I had my eye on the gun my man was holding on me, but I didn't know if Heather was tuned in to the possibility of moving against them. In the next second, I found out.

'Nick!' she shouted, and chopped sidewise at the thin man's gun hand. His revolver clattered to the sidewalk as Heather hit him again, this time in the face.

In the meantime, I'd kicked out at the soccer player's knee and connected with a loud crack. He yelled and doubled over, grabbing the leg. While he was distracted, I grabbed for his gun.

Heather now had a good hold on the thin man. She let his own momentum carry him off-balance then, using her body as a lever, threw him violently across the hood of the Rolls. He landed on his back.

Heather moved after the gun he'd dropped but had trouble locating it. I was still trying to wrestle the gun away from the soccer player who was putting up quite a fight.

I heard Heather shout, 'Got it!' as she finally came up with the thin man's gun . . . too late.

'Drop it or I'll blow a bleeding hole through you.' The driver of the Rolls had joined the act with a big ugly revolver he was holding aimed at Heather's back.

Heather groaned, glanced over at me and saw that I was in no position to help and dropped the gun.

'Now,' the driver said, swinging his gun toward me, 'you stay right there. You come here, birdie.'

Heather moved to him. He slapped her hard and almost knocked her down. 'Turn and put your arms behind you,' he said.

He nodded to the thin man who'd limped over to retrieve the gun Heather had dropped. He came over, took a pair of handcuffs from his back pocket and slipped them around Heather's slender wrists. She gasped as he pressed them closed, far too tight. I cursed him under my breath.

The driver came over to me now. He was a heavy man with a slightly flabby face. He gave me a very nasty look and swung his revolver against my head. I grunted and went down, bleeding from a cut forehead. Then he and the soccer player jerked my hands behind me and locked a pair of cuffs on my wrists. They hauled me to my feet and shoved me into the Rolls. The thin man pushed Heather in beside me.

We drove for over an hour, the lights of London gradually fading behind us. It was black night when we turned into the drive of a country estate and the

Rolls stopped at the main door of a large stone house. The three thugs got out of the car.

'All right, you two. Out.' The thin man was giving the orders again.

They dragged us out of the back seat. 'Inside,' the thin man said, indicating the house.

The place was very elegant, with the look and feel of Old England. We stepped into a high-ceilinged reception hall. Lights were on but nobody met us.

'He said to take them to the tower,' the driver reminded the others.

They marched us along a corridor to a narrow circular stairwell. It had a dank, musty smell. We climbed slowly up worn stone steps by the light of dim bulbs set at sparse intervals. At the top, the thin man stuck an iron key into the rusty lock of a heavy oak door and pushed the door open. We entered a circular stone room with a single barred window.

'Well, this is it. Rest well.' The thin man grinned.

There was no furniture in the room.

'How about taking the cuffs off the girl?' I asked.

The thin man turned back to me. 'Cuffs off the bird, you say?'

'That's right,' I said. 'Look how red her wrists are, you're cutting the circulation off.'

'Ah! Circulation, is it?' he said. 'Is that what's worrying you?'

He hauled off and slugged me. I dropped to one knee and he kicked me in the side. I grunted and fell over.

'There you are, Yank!' he said. 'That should improve your ruddy circulation!' He laughed and so did the soccer player. The driver just looked bored.

They left the room. We heard the key turn in the lock and then their footsteps, growng fainter and fainter, as they went back down the stairs.

Ten

'I'm sorry, love. I just can't manage it.'

'It's all right,' I said. Heather moved away from me and slumped to the floor, her back against the wall. She was very pale and looked completely exhausted.

'We've been in this bloody place for hours and hours now,' she said angrily. She had just been attempting, for the sixth time, to unfasten the difficult clasp on the buckle of my belt but her hands were too swollen, she just could not manipulate them well enough, and we needed that belt and the buckle.

'I'm sorry, baby,' I said.

'Do you think anyone will ever come?' she asked.

'I don't know,' I admitted. 'Maybe Jupiter intends to let us die up here but somehow I doubt it. I think he wants to find out how much we know first.'

It was daylight; a warm sun filtered through the high barred window in the wall, but the heavy oak door remained shut.

I looked down again at the belt and buckle that Special Effects and Editing had supplied me with. It contained plastic explosives and a tiny disassembled blowgun, but if I couldn't get it off, it was of no use.

'I'm thirsty,' Heather said.

I opened my mouth to reply when I heard something on the stairs. It grew louder. Someone was coming up. 'Listen,' I said, 'we have visitors.'

A moment later, the key turned in the lock and the door swung open. Elmo Jupiter stood in the doorway, tall and imposing. The driver of the Rolls-Royce stood behind him with a gun.

'Well!' Jupiter said brightly. 'We meet again. And so soon.'

Heather's eyes darkened. 'You bloody bastard!'

Jupiter clucked his tongue. 'Such language for a lady.' He moved into the room. 'I hope you've found the accommodation comfortable.'

'If you ever had any feeling for Heather,' I said grimly, 'you'll bring her some water. And loosen those damned cuffs.'

He regarded me coldly. 'How delighted I am that you accepted my invitation too,' he said smoothly.

'You who have made such a determined effort to wreck my plan.'

'I didn't succeed,' I told him. 'Your money should be in Switzerland by now. Haven't they told you?'

'They've told me,' he said. 'I gave your people further instructions, but they haven't acted on them.' He pushed his big hand through his dark blond hair. The scar stood out vividly on his neck. 'Could it be that SOE is playing cat and mouse with me – Mr Carter?'

So he knew my true identity. Jupiter's underground intelligence network was certainly top-notch. I could see that he was waiting for my reaction, so I ignored it completely. 'Nobody's playing games, Jupiter. But SOE may doubt your motives since we've disappeared. What do you hope to accomplish? Are you doing this for the money, or do you just enjoy killing?'

He laughed at that. 'They taught me how to kill and I refined the practice to an art.' Suddenly the smile was gone and a different mood struck him. 'Yes, I enjoy killing when it removes the leeches from my flesh. I tried to play their game but they held all the high cards you see. Now they must play by *my* rules. And they must pay, Mr Carter, in more ways than one. Does that answer your question?'

'Explicitly,' I said. 'Just one more question: how did Fergus know you were the assassin?'

Jupiter looked at me dumbly. 'Fergus? Who's Fergus?'

'Augie Fergus. He was in your commando unit.'

Jupiter's eyes lit up with recognition. 'Ah, yes. Fergus. I remember him now. Good night fighter.' Then he snapped his fingers in recall. 'The hospital. Of course. He was wounded in the same action I was. Occupied the bed next to mine. Most of the time we had nothing to do but talk about where we'd go after the war. I remember now. That was when the germ of my plan was born. We were discussing all sorts of ways a man could make a million pounds, and I said how easy it would be to extort the money from the government. Just kill a few cabinet ministers, then demand . . . oh, I don't remember the figure . . . for the safety of the rest. You say Fergus knew John Elmore is the assassin? He must have remembered the conversation, then put two and two together. But that doesn't matter now, does it, Mr Carter?'

'You've got the money,' I said. 'Let us go and show the government your good faith.'

Jupiter started to smile again, but suddenly his face switched and a reflection of pain showed in his cold eyes. He raised his hand to the side of his head.

'The plate,' he said harshly. 'It causes pain at times. And they are responsible for it, those men who sit in the government. What were they doing during the war, Mr Carter? While I was having the top of my skull blown off, what were they doing?'

His eyes grew wilder as he continued. 'I'll tell you what they were doing. They were sitting in the safety of London. And those same men – how did they repay me for my services? By taxing my business to the limit. Everything I own, all the money I made, went into that business. And now it is on the verge of bankruptcy. It is their fault,' he was raging now, 'all their fault. But they will pay,' he chuckled madly. 'They will pay dearly. And the two of you will pay dearly for the difficulties you have caused me. That is why I had you brought here rather than killed immediately. You gave me a very large headache when you barged into my plant with your ridiculous story. The tour was free then, Mr Carter, but you will pay for it now. You and this lovely creature.' He looked hungrily at Heather. 'I have plans for you, my dear.' He bent down and ran a hand along her thigh; she tried to move away from him.

Anger had been building inside me and when Jupiter touched Heather, it exploded. I came off the floor awkwardly and threw myself at him, knocking him backwards. 'Leave her alone, you bastard!' I yelled.

Jupiter's face hardened and madness glinted behind the eyes. The man on the landing moved closer with the gun.

'No!' Jupiter told him.

He closed the distance between us. He was as tall as I and looked as hard as nails. Suddenly he jabbed his fist into my stomach, just under the heart. I grunted in pain as the breath was knocked out of me. I fell back against the wall, Jupiter moving in after me.

I kicked out at his groin but he side-stepped and I caught his thigh instead. He delivered a hard chop over my right ear. I slumped to one knee but managed to stagger back to my feet. Jupiter came at me again. This time the edge of his hand struck me on the neck, the paralyzing blow knocking me to the floor.

'Don't!' I heard Heather scream.

The kick got me in the side. I let out a yell, my whole body aflame with pain. My hands struggled automatically against the handcuffs holding them. I wished as much as I had ever wished for anything that they were free and locked around Jupiter's throat.

He stood over me, breathing heavily. 'I'll have more time for you later,' he growled.

'This – sort of thing isn't going to – get you your fourteen million pounds,' I gasped.

'How kind of you to worry about me, old fellow,' Jupiter said acidly. 'But I'll get the money and my satisfaction. I've already warned them about further delay. Now I'm going to show them how determined I am. There is going to be a fourth assassination, ahead of schedule.'

Heather and I stared at him. His eyes shone brightly and his cheeks were flushed in an ugly way. Elmo Jupiter looked like what he was: a madman.

'It will be a really big fish this time,' he said, smiling again. 'And there will be others caught in the same net. Well, I've warned them.'

'Don't do it,' I said. 'Let us contact our superiors and we'll set things straight about the money. I'm sure it's only a misunderstanding.'

'Misunderstanding, yes,' he said. 'Of Elmo Jupiter.

When I promise to kill, Mr Carter, I kill. I never make empty threats.' He paused to offer that psychotic grin. 'Perhaps it will give you something to think about, Mr Carter, to know that I propose to kill you. Very slowly.'

I shrugged with an elaborate unconcern I did not feel. 'If that's the way you want it. But why not ease off on Heather in the meantime? Look at her hands.'

Jupiter's sparkling eyes turned from me to Heather. He nodded to the man with the gun.

Heather's cuffs came off. She rubbed her wrists to get the circulation going.

'Now put the cuffs on her only not so tightly,' Jupiter said. He wasn't taking any chances. 'Are Mr Carter's cuffs tight?' he asked. The flunky checked them and nodded. 'Good,' Jupiter said. 'Leave them that way.'

He gave us a parting grin, then he and his man were gone.

When we could no longer hear them on the stairs, I turned to Heather. 'Who do you think Jupiter has marked off now?'

'The Prime Minister, I'm afraid,' she said. 'But surely he can't get past the massive security!'

'He's done it twice before, not counting Wellsey,' I said. 'Damn, we have to get out of this place. It's obvious this isn't listed in Jupiter's name or Brutus would have been here by now.'

'We're off toward Oxford somewhere,' Heather said. 'I could tell that much from watching where they drove,' she said. 'Maybe around Beaconsfield. There are a number of large estates in the area.'

I moved over closer to her and looked at her hands. The metal cuffs were no longer cutting into her flesh but her hands were swollen. 'Knead your hands,' I said. 'Rub them together.'

'They're very sore, Nick.'

'I know. But if we can get the swelling down, we'll try working on my belt buckle again. With your fingers functioning properly, you may be able to unsnap the clasp.'

'All right,' she said obediently. 'I'll knead.'

The hours passed. Soon the light through the small opening in the oak door exceeded the feeble sunlight coming through the barred window. It was almost dark outside.

The swelling had gradually gone down; Heather's hands were almost back to normal.

'Do you want to try the buckle again now?' I asked. 'Or wait?'

Heather rubbed her hands behind her. 'They feel fairly good, Nick. But I can't promise anything.'

'I know,' I said. 'But let's try.'

She backed up to me and found my belt. 'Yes, higher,' I told her. 'Now pull the buckle toward you. Right. I can see the damned catch despite this lousy light. Now, move your index finger to your left.'

'That's it, isn't it?'

'Right. Now it has to be pushed to your right.'

'I remember. But the bloody thing is stuck somehow, Nick. Or else I'm doing it all wrong.'

'Keep trying. Try depressing the button slightly before pushing it to the right.'

I heard her grunt as she manipulated her hands awkwardly behind her. Suddenly, miraculously, there was a tiny clicking noise and I felt the belt loosen. I looked down and Heather turned her head questioningly.

'You did it!' I told her.

Heather took hold of the buckle and pulled the belt off. She turned back to me, holding the belt behind her. 'Now what?'

'Now we turn back to back again and I open the back of the buckle, hopefully, using the same catch but this time moving it downward. We can use the blowgun for a lock pick, if I can get at it. The trouble will be avoiding the small dart. If I break the plastic wrapper on the tip accidentally and prick myself, the ball game will be over – it's poisoned.'

My back to Heather's, I reached out for the buckle. I found the catch and, after some difficulty, moved it in the right direction. The back of the buckle popped off. I felt around inside gingerly, touched the dart and shied away from it. Then my fumbling fingers touched the larger-diametered half of the tiny two-part blowgun. Carefully I removed the other, narrower part from the buckle and twisted awkwardly to look at it.

'Okay,' I told Heather. 'Drop the belt and hold your cuffs close to my hands.'

I touched the handcuffs and fumbled for the lock. With great difficulty I managed to insert the slender metal tube I was holding into the lock.

'This is going to be tricky,' I said. 'Hold as still as possible.'

Working behind yourself and upside down, in a twisted, uncomfortable position, is not the easiest way to pick a lock. Just trying to keep in mind in what direction to move the pick against the tumbler was a challenge. But after fifteen minutes of it, the lock clicked and Heather's cuffs were loose. I sighed a heavy sigh of relief as she moved away and pulled her hands from the cuffs.

'Now *you* have to do it for me,' I told her.

She moved around in back of me.

For her it was an easier job. Her hands were free and she could see what she was doing. In a few minutes she had my cuffs unlocked.

I dropped them to the floor.

Working quickly, in almost complete darkness now, I ripped the belt open. It was lined with explosives in plastic form, like putty. There was also a short fuse and a match. I wadded the plastic into a ball and stuck the fuse into it. Then I assembled the four-inch blowgun and unwrapped the tiny dart.

'Well,' I said. 'We're ready, I guess. We have nothing to pick the door lock with so we'll have to blow it.'

'But there's no place to get away from the explosion,' Heather pointed out.

'I know. Lie down against the wall near the door, opposite the lock.' I moved to the door and jammed the plastic against the lock; it stuck there, the fuse extending out of it toward me. 'Cover your ears and head,' I told Heather, 'and open your mouth.'

I took the match out. 'Well, this is it,' I said. I struck the match and touched it to the fuse. I saw it start, then dived onto Heather, covering my head.

The explosion was not a loud one as explosions go, but it seemed thunderous in that small room. Our ears rang and our heads hurt and I was hit in the back with a sharp piece of flying wood. We staggered to our feet while the smoke was still clearing. The door stood open.

'That will bring anyone who's downstairs,' I said.

And it did. They came rushing up the stairs. Heather stood on one side of the door and I stood on the other. There were two of them. Heather had the blowgun and was ready to use it. The first man to appear in the dim light of the landing was the thin gunman we had met before. He hesitated a second, then moved into the room.

I took him; I struck viciously at his gunhand, knocking the gun loose. Then I grabbed his arm, jerking him off his feet into the room. I met him in the middle of the floor as he struggled up, smashed a hard right into his face. The bone snapped in his nose and he spun heavily against the opposite wall.

The second man, the Rolls driver, was at the door now, aiming his gun at me. Heather raised the blowgun and sent the dart on its way. It struck him in the neck, buried half of its shaft. Startled, he forgot about shooting me. He plucked the dart out, looked at it, and suddenly his eyes rolled and he fell flat on his face in the doorway.

I delivered a karate chop to the thin man's larynx. He made a gurgling sound and collapsed.

'Let's get out of here!' I grabbed Heather by the elbow.

We dived down the circular staircase. We met no one else coming up and as we made our way along the ground floor toward the front door, the house appeared to be empty. We searched the rooms we passed quickly. No one. But I did find our guns and Hugo in a desk in the library.

There was a car in the drive but the keys weren't in it. I reached under the dash, crossed wires to start it. We slammed the doors shut and roared off.

'We have to get to Brutus,' I said, as we turned out of the drive onto the main road.

'Let's hope we're not too late,' Heather said.

Brutus strode up and down in front of his desk. He didn't have the pipe in his teeth for a change and that seemed to make him more excitable.

'What does the bloody devil want from us?' he said loudly. 'He sent instructions which were very ambiguous about delivering the money in Switzerland. We needed clarification and couldn't get it. And then your disappearance made us wonder what the chap was really up to. Jupiter's office and home are under surveillance but he hasn't been to either place since you were kidnapped.'

'He probably won't go back to that country place now either,' I said. 'And I think he's set on another assassination no matter what we do about the money.'

Brutus had called the Prime Minister when we explained why we thought he might be Jupiter's next target. Brutus and the P.M. had agreed that the most likely occasion for the attempt would be at a foreign ministers' conference at the Ministry, the day after tomorrow.

'Will Sir Leslie call off the conference, do you think?' I asked.

Brutus sighed. 'I'm afraid that Sir Leslie does not have the same regard for his own life that he has for other people's safety. He keeps talking about the importance of the conference and pointing out how tight security is now. He's to call me back after he confers with his other advisors. I told him, of course, to scrap the bloody conference until this thing blows over.'

'Is Scotland Yard trying to locate Jupiter?' I asked.

'They're everywhere,' Brutus said. 'They've questioned everybody at Jupiter's plant and people he has been seen with socially. Our agents and MI5 and 6 are on it too, of course. But Mr Jupiter has disappeared. We've sent men to the house you were taken to, but I'm sure it's too late.'

'I imagine he'll turn up day after tomorrow,' I said.

Brutus looked over at me glumly. 'Yes, I daresay. Let's hope Sir Leslie decides to play it safe.' He sat down at his desk. 'Incidentally, I had to inform David Hawk when you two disappeared. He was very concerned about you. I'm to contact him now that you're back.'

A buzzer sounded on Brutus' desk. 'Oh, yes,' he said, answering it. He flipped a switch and stood up. 'It's Sir Leslie. I'll take it in the next room.'

Heather got up from the corner of the desk, crushed a cigarette into an ashtray and moved over to me.

She was just about to kiss me when Brutus walked back in again.

'Well, that's it,' he said, tensely, his big British Army chin jutting out grimly. 'Sir Leslie will have the bloody conference, on schedule.' He shook his head. 'It appears we have our work cut out.'

Eleven

It was the afternoon of the ministers' conference. The morning had passed uneventfully and already the Yard and MI5 were saying that SOE had guessed wrong – there would be no assassination attempt, not today, not here.

I was positive there would be. The foreign ministers' conference was the perfect setup. If some of the ministers got killed along with Sir Leslie, Britain would not only lose her head of state but would suffer great international embarrassment. Jupiter would enjoy that.

I had not seen Heather since before the noon recess

when we met at a cafeteria and had a sandwich together. Brutus had given us free rein on this security assignment, letting us move around as we liked and do what we thought was most important at the moment. Heather had spent much of the morning in the conference room while I patrolled the corridors of the building. I had resumed that activity now and she had accompanied the conference members to a luncheon served in another part of the building.

If Jupiter had been telling the truth about catching 'other fish' in his fourth assassination attempt, all kinds of possibilities opened up regarding the method he might use. A tommy gun, for instance, or a small bomb or a grenade or poison gas.

The air conditioning system had been checked out by experts several times but I'd checked it myself again during the morning session. Teams of bomb and demoliton experts had gone over the conference room before the morning session and during a mid-morning break and found nothing. The security men were beginning to relax and joke about the whole business.

I wasn't laughing; they didn't know Jupiter. Our failure to find anything so far probably only meant we hadn't looked in the right place – and Jupiter was likely to have the last laugh.

I came to the big doors of the conference room and was stopped by two MI5 men and a policeman.

'SOE,' I said, showing them my I.D.

They checked the card with extreme care and finally

let me pass. I moved into the room and looked around. Everything appeared normal. There was a spotter over at a window, watching nearby rooftops, a policeman with a pair of powerful binoculars. I went over to him and leaned on the sill of the open window as a security helicopter fluttered by overhead.

'May I have a look?' I asked the bobby.

'Don't mind if you do,' he said, handing the glasses to me.

I studied the nearest rooftops. They were crawling with security people so there seemed little point in watching them. I refocused the glasses for infinity and scanned the further horizon. I focused on a broad roof with several rises of superstructure and saw movement there. A dark haired man was walking about, probably a policeman. Yes, I could make out the uniform now.

I sighed and handed the glasses back. 'Thanks,' I said.

I moved back out into the corridor. The ministers were returning from the luncheon, straggling down the hall. The afternoon session, which was getting a late start, would soon be in progress.

I left the area and moved up to the roof, stopping to show my I.D. several times. Security certainly seemed tight, but remembering how easily Jupiter had gained access to the Foreign Minister's office, I wasn't reassured.

I met Heather on the roof. She was carrying a walkie-talkie with which she could communicate with the temporary SOE command post.

'Hello, Nick.' She smiled at me. 'Is everything quiet downstairs?'

'So far.' I put my arm around her shoulders. 'I wish I could figure him out, Heather. He's giving me an inferiority complex. If he's around today, he's –'

I stopped and stared at a man who was moving past us. He wore a white serving jacket and was carrying a plate of sandwiches. He was tall with dark hair and built like Jupiter. I grabbed his arm and reached for Wilhelmina.

The man turned, fear in his face when he saw the gun. The hair was real, he had a hooked nose and he was obviously genuine.

'Eh, what's this, gov'nor?' he said.

'Nothing,' I said, embarrassed. 'Sorry. Go ahead – it was a mistake.'

He muttered something and hurried on. A couple of agents nearby who'd witnessed the scene grinned.

'I must be getting jumpy,' I told Heather, wryly. 'Although you've got to admit a waiter would be a good disguise and, after all, Jupiter did crash the Foreign Secretary's offices as a janitor. Still, this poor guy doesn't look like him at all. Except for the dark hair and the serving jacket –'

I stopped: the jacket ... a uniform ... dark hair ...

I turned and looked out over the city toward the buildings to the west. I moved quickly to a spotter busy watching other policemen on the next roof through his binoculars.

'Let me borrow those a moment,' I said, raising my voice to be heard above the flutter of another passing helicopter.

'All right. But you could ask a bit nicer,' he said.

I didn't answer him. I took the binoculars and refocused them on the distant building with all the superstructures I had noticed from the conference room. I had more of a vantage point here; I could see the rooftop quite clearly. There was no movement there now. I was looking slightly down on the roof and now I noticed something set up there. As I readjusted the glasses, my mouth went dry. I was looking at what appeared to be a weapon of some kind, perhaps a mortar, and it was aimed at me.

Then I saw movement again. It was the man in the policeman's uniform but this time I noticed the dark hair and the mustache and the tall, square build. It was Jupiter.

The foreign ministers' meeting was back in session downstairs, and that damned weapon was aimed right at the windows of the conference room! Of course. Jupiter had no intention of trying to gain entrance to the Ministry building this time. He was going to make use of his excellent military training to strike from a distance.

I handed the glasses back to the spotter roughly. 'Thanks,' I said. I hurried over to Heather. 'Get an identification of that building,' I said, pointing. 'Call Brutus and tell him that Jupiter is on the roof with a medium-distance weapon. Then go to the conference room and try to convince somebody to break it up. Another thing: Radio a helicopter to stand by in case Jupiter gets away. I'm going after him.'

It was a hectic race on foot to the other building several blocks away. The sidewalks were jammed with pedestrians and I kept running into people. A cab almost knocked me down as I crossed a side street. At last I was there. The building turned out to be a hotel.

I waited an interminable time for an elevator and took it to the top floor. Then I raced to the stairs leading to the roof. I came out not twenty yards from Jupiter.

He was bending over his weapon, getting ready to fire it. Three wicked-looking rockets lay beside it. A rocket mortar. With three shells Jupiter couldn't help hitting the conference room. One properly aimed shell would destroy the room and everyone in it.

'Hold it!' I yelled, drawing Wilhelmina.

He whirled toward me. 'You again!' he snarled. He pulled a Browning Parabellum automatic out of his belt and ducked behind the mortar. I flattened myself against the wall behind me as Jupiter fired. The slug chipped cement beside my head, showering me with a fine gray powder. I returned fire with the Luger and the slug clanged off the barrel of the mortar.

There was another service superstructure close to Jupiter. He pulled off another shot at me, missing widely, and raced for cover. I fired as he ran but missed, chipping the roof at his feet.

'It's all over, Jupiter,' I yelled. 'Give it up.'

Jupiter leaned out from behind his cover and fired. This time the slug nicked my left arm, tearing a hole in my jacket. I grabbed the arm and swore.

Jupiter was back behind cover now. I started to circle, away from his line of vision. Moving carefully, I rounded the superstructure and there was Jupiter, not fifteen feet away.

Unfortunately, my foot scraped some gravel on the roof, and Jupiter heard me. He whirled and fired automatically, and I ducked back. I heard him running then and when I looked out around the corner, I saw him making for the mortar. He reached it, stuck his gun in his belt and picked up a rocket. The weapon was obviously already aimed.

I could not risk firing and not killing him. I shoved Wilhelmina into my belt and raced toward him. The rocket disappeared inside the cannon and I hit Jupiter and the weapon simultaneously. The mortar roared and the rocket flashed into the London sky, but I had knocked the barrel on an angle.

The rocket sizzled out over the city, missed the Ministry building completely and exploded in a small park area near it. In the moment I took to watch the rocket's progress, Jupiter smashed a fist into my face and twisted away from me. Then he was back on his feet. 'Damn you, Carter!' He had the Browning out again and aimed at me. He fired and I rolled; the slug zinged harmlessly off the concrete edge of the roof behind me.

Jupiter did not try a second shot. A helicopter fluttered in and dropped down, hovering a few feet above the roof. I thought, gratefully, that it was the police chopper – until I saw the ladder being lowered for Jupiter. He was on it now and climbing; the helicopter was already moving away.

I fired but Jupiter was already scrambling inside the cabin and I missed.

Looking out over the rooftops, I saw another 'copter moving toward me. I fired a shot and waved it down. This one did belong to the police. It hovered a moment, then dropped to the roof. I ran over, ducking under the whirling blades, the wind they stirred tugging at me.

There was the pilot and Heather inside. I jumped in and pointed to the departed chopper, heading southwest out of town. 'Follow it,' I said.

We lifted off the roof and made a banking turn, heading out after Jupiter. We were flying into a setting sun and his 'copter was silhouetted against a peach-colored sky.

Our speed increased and, as we moved into open country we closed in on the other 'copter. The pilot had radioed back to the Yard about what was happening, but I knew it would probably all be up to us.

We were within a hundred yards of the other 'copter and I aimed the Luger, wishing I had a rifle, and fired a couple of shots. I hit the 'copter but I didn't do any damage. I could see Jupiter and the pilot clearly.

The sun had almost set now. If night fell before we caught them, they would be able to lose us easily. I turned to the pilot.

'Open it up!' I yelled.

The distance closed a little more. We were a long way from London now, heading in the direction of Andover. A thatched-roof village passed below us and we drew a little closer; the distance between us was not much more than fifty yards. I leaned out and fired again. This time I hit the gas tank but the fuel did not ignite it. It would leak out though. I expected Jupiter to return fire, but for some reason he didn't. Maybe he was conserving ammo.

'He'll have to land now, sir,' my pilot said.

'Let's hope so.'

The pilot was right. In a minute, Jupiter's 'copter started down toward a small village below. We followed. They landed in a field on the outskirts of the village beside a commercial building that turned out to be a motor-cycle garage.

'Set us down,' I told my pilot. 'But don't give him a good shot at us – he's an expert.'

Jupiter's 'copter was down and he was climbing out. We set down about sixty yards away. I was reloading the Luger, but my pilot cut the engine and jumped to the ground impatiently.

'Keep down!' I yelled at him.

But it was too late. Jupiter fired and hit him in the chest, twisting him violently off his feet. By the time I reached the ground, Jupiter was heading toward a half-dozen motorcycles sitting outside the garage. I examined the pilot's wound; it was bad but he would live if he got help in time. I ordered Heather to stay with him, then jumped to my feet.

I started running in a crouch toward the garage where Jupiter was mounting a cycle. I was so intent on catching up with him I forgot about his chopper pilot until a slug whistled past my ear. I spotted the man then, returned fire with Wilhelmina and hit him. He staggered backward and fell; he didn't get up.

I kept running. Jupiter had started the cycle and was turning it toward the road fronting the place.

I stopped, rested Wilhelmina on my forearm and fired, but Jupiter was roaring off down the road. He was riding a BSA Victor Special 441, with the long narrow seat and the gas tank up between seat and handlebars. I figured it had a top speed of eighty miles an hour.

I moved quickly to a man standing, pale and shaken, just inside the garage. 'Police,' I said because it was easiest. 'What do you have here that will beat that Victor?'

He pointed to a big old bike, long and heavy; it was a 1958 Ariel 4G Square Four.

'Take the Squariel,' he said. 'It's an old timer but it has fifty horsepower, four speeds and will hit almost a hundred.'

'Thanks,' I said. I moved to the machine and climbed on. I started it with a hard kick. As the engine roared, I shouted to the garage man: 'I'll settle later.

Get a doctor for my friend in the field. The other one doesn't need help.'

He nodded. I gunned the bike and roared away, up the narrow road after Jupiter.

There was a pair of goggles on the handlebars and I put them on, swinging around a shrub-lined curve. I didn't bother to keep to the left but used the whole road. I had to catch Jupiter and I knew he was pushing his bike to the limit.

It was dark now, and I switched on the lights. There was no one ahead of me. Suddenly, a pair of headlights appeared in my rear-view mirror. They swiftly loomed larger, than an MG sedan drew up to me. Behind the driver's seat was Heather. She must have commandeered the car after seeing to the wounded pilot.

I accelerated, trying to keep up with her, but her machine was too powerful for my Ariel. Then, somewhere in the distance I heard the tortured squeal of brakes and a sickening crash. A lump caught in my throat. The crash was too loud for a motorcycle. It had to have been Heather.

I passed her overturned MG up the road just past a curve. It was wrapped halfway around a tree. The wheels were still spinning eerily. I slowed, determined that no one could have survived that crash. Heather, in her less maneuverable vehicle, must have attempted to take the curve at the same speed Jupiter had. Only she hadn't made it.

Blind hatred caused the blood to pound in my

ears. Until now, Jupiter had been just another opponent. Now he was something more: Heather's murderer.

I drove for several miles, watching the side road. Just when I was sure Jupiter had given me the slip, I rounded a curve and there he was, not two hundred yards ahead of me. He was running without lights.

He turned and saw me coming up on him. His speed increased somewhat but I was still closing in. He disappeared around a curve and I lost him for several minutes in a series of blind turns. On the next straightaway I found him again, only a hundred yards ahead. He turned and fired wildly at me twice. It was ridiculous at that speed and in the dark. I had closed to fifty yards now.

Suddenly, Jupiter turned into a dirt road to the left, kicking up a long cloud of dust in the darkness. I managed to stop the Ariel just in time, skidding its rear end around as I roared down the road after Jupiter.

A half mile and we crossed a small arched wooden bridge. Our momentum lifted the bikes into the air on the far side of the bridge and dropped us back down hard. Jupiter almost lost control when he hit, his bike weaving wildly. The Ariel was heavier and I held it better. A couple of hundred yards later, we crossed the same stream by a natural ford, splashing through the shallow water and sending it up in sheets on both sides of the bikes. There was a steep hill-climb on the far side of soft sand. My Ariel squirmed around in the soft stuff for a moment, then broke free.

On the other side of the hill, Jupiter made a sharp left turn and headed out into open country. I followed, hoping the Ariel wasn't too big for the job. Jupiter gained some ground on me over the next couple of miles, bumping wildly over hillocks, into ruts and dodging small trees. Then we topped a low rise, and suddenly I knew where we were. Before us on a flat plain, only a few hundred yards away, stood an eerie circle of towering flat stones, dark and massive against the lighter sky. We were riding toward the ancient archaeological site of Stonehenge, either by accident or by Jupiter's design.

Whichever it was, it was clear that Jupiter intended to make his stand here. He had already reached the spot and as I closed the distance to a hundred yards, he dismounted and let his cycle drop. Then he moved quickly toward the ancient ceremonial ruin.

I stopped my cycle and turned the engine off. I got off and stood facing the forbidding ruin warily. Stonehenge was an ancient pre-Druid temple, erected for worship of the sun and moon, geared in its design to measure the movements of the heavenly bodies. What was left of it was actually a circle of massive cut stones set inside a circle of similar stones, plus a few outlying markers. Some of the stones were in pairs with a third lying across the tops to form a primitive arch or lintel. The sun and moon rose and set through those arches on particular days of the year converting the temple into a gigantic sidereal clock. But none of that interested me at the moment because there was a madman hidden here now, intent on killing me.

I moved slowly toward that ring of giant stones, watching the shadows. The sky was clear but the moon was not up yet so there was little light. The night was completely silent.

I moved to an isolated stone and stopped, searching the darkness. Then Jupiter's voice came from somewhere in the shadows, ahead of me.

'Now, Mr Carter, you're playing on my home court,' he said. 'Being an American, I suppose you're not overly familiar with Stonehenge. You're standing by the ancient Slaughter Stone. Isn't that appropriate?' A shot whined off the rock inches from my head.

I ducked down and saw Jupiter's figure leave the cover of a massive stone and run to another. I fired twice and hit nothing. I moved to another set of stone and stopped to listen. I heard Jupiter's unnerving, quiet laughter:

'It's a fascinating place, Mr Carter. Did you know, for instance, that it's just thirteen steps between the trilithons on this side of the circle?' The shadow moved again and Jupiter took running steps to the next bulky silhouette. Again I fired after him and again I missed. The light simply wasn't good enough.

'It also might interest you,' Jupiter's tight, high voice came again, 'that the angle formed by the Altar Stone here, the trilithon beside you, and the distant Heel Stone is forty-five degrees and that you're in line with the Heel Stone.' Another shot; the slug tore past my left shoulder.

I ducked and swore. I was beginning to understand why Jupiter had chosen the place to make his stand. Here he could not only kill me but also enjoy the formalities of the execution. I moved quickly to another large stone, out of his range of fire. He already had me on the defensive.

'I'm maneuvering you, Mr Carter,' he called out. 'How does it feel to be the mouse for a change instead of the cat?'

The Browning automatic fired again. I jerked back and ran for what appeared to be a safe location. Suddenly shadows began changing and a growing light brightened the ground. At that moment, Jupiter called out from cover nearby:

'Excellent, Mr Carter! You're just where I want you. The great clock is working against you behind your back.'

I glanced behind me and saw what he meant. I was standing under the arch of the famous Moonrise Trilithon which was at right angles to the Heel Stone. Jupiter had manipulated me, all right. A full moon was rising behind me, the brilliant light made me a perfect target.

I turned back to Jupiter – too late. He was standing out in the open, his Browning aimed at my chest.

'Goodbye, Mr Carter!'

He was taking time with the final stages of the execution. He sighted along the barrel and slowly tightened his trigger finger. I closed my eyes, and a shot reverberated in the night. But I wasn't hit. I opened my eyes. Standing next to a stone pillar, her Sterling PPL in her hand, was Heather. She had escaped the crash alive, and it was her shot I had heard.

Jupiter cursed loudly, swung the Browning in her direction and fired once. But Heather had ducked behind the pillar and the bullet ricochetted harmlessly off the stone. With a lightning movement Jupiter swung the Browning back to me. He pulled the trigger before I could react, but the only sound was a loud click as the hammer fell on an empty chamber. Jupiter had played the cat-and-mouse game too long.

He swore violently and threw the gun to the ground. I aimed the Luger at him as he dived for the ground. My shot dug into the calf of his right leg. But when I tried to fire Wilhelmina again, I discovered that I, too, had run out of ammunition.

Realising what had happened, Jupiter picked up the short wooden pole, one of several lying around left by workers on some archaeological team probably, and limped toward me. I holstered Wilhelmina and picked up a pole of my own just as Jupiter reached me. He slammed the pole down toward my head. I deflected the blow at the last moment with my pole.

'A little knightly joust perhaps?' Jupiter said, breathing hard. In the light of the moon, I could see the mad glitter in his eyes.

He swung the pole again, with both hands, using it as the ancient Britons had, staggering a little on his wounded leg. His madness gave him strength. Again I found myself on the defensive. He swung at me again and this time connected with a glancing blow to the side of my head. I stumbled backwards and fell.

Jupiter pressed his advantage, swinging for my head. I tried to parry the blow but still the club thudded into my arm and chest, knocking the pole out of my hand.

I rolled away from the next blow and as Jupiter raised the pole again, I twitched the muscle in my right forearm. Hugo slipped into my palm.

The pole was coming toward my head again when Hugo sank into Jupiter's heart. He stopped, the pole stretched out in front of him, staring at me in sudden bewilderment and frustration. He raised the pole slightly, took one uncertain step toward me, then did a half-spin to the left and collapsed.

I took a deep breath and let it out slowly. It was over. I pulled Hugo from Jupiter's body and wiped the blade off on his trousers. Then I returned the stiletto to its sheath. I looked at Jupiter in the light of the rising moon.

Heather came up to me and put her arm around my waist. She was shivering. 'The distance was too great. I knew I couldn't hit him. I only fired to distract him,' she whispered.

I gathered her close to me. 'You saved my life, you

know,' I said. 'That last bullet he fired at you, it was meant for me. If it hadn't been for you . . . '

She shuddered and sought the warmth of my body.

'Anyway, I have to admit you're one hell of an agent. I had my doubts at the beginning, but you're quite something, as an agent . . . and as a girl.'

'That's how I'm best,' she smiled up at me. 'As a girl, I mean,' she said, reaching for my hand.

She clasped my hand in hers and drew me along to the tall grass which surrounded Stonehenge. We sank into the dew-covered earth and she began proving to me again just how good she was . . . as a girl.

Nick Carter in an unbeatable spy adventure series

Westerns in Tandem editions

The Wild Bunch Brian Fox	25p
A Dollar to Die For Brian Fox	30p
For a Few Dollars More Joe Millard	30p
The Good, The Bad and The Ugly Joe Millard	30p
Valdez is Coming Elmore Leonard	25p
The McMasters Dean Owen	25p
Lawman Grant Freeling	25p
Sabata Brian Fox	25p
Macho Callahan Joe Millard	25p
The Hunting Party Joe Millard	25p
A Coffin Full of Dollars Joe Millard	25p
Chato's Land Joe Millard	25p
The Valdez Horses Lee Hoffman	30p
A Fistful of Dynamite James Lewis	30p
The Devil's Dollar Sign Joe Millard	30p

U.F.O.s in Tandem editions

Flying Saucers from Outer Space Donald E. Keyhoe	30p
Flying Saucers are Hostile Brad Steiger & Joan Whritenour	25p
Strangers from the Skies Brad Steiger	25p
The Sky People Brinsley Le Poer Trench	25p

Science Fiction in Tandem editions

Planet of No Return Poul Anderson `..    ..    ..` 25p
    Man must search for colonies beyond the stars, but
    can he find a permanent home there?

The Time-Hoppers Robert Silverberg `..    ..    ..` 25p
    Every human need was fulfilled in the 25th century,
    yet they still yearned to escape

Hawksbill Station Robert Silverberg `..    ..    ..` 25p
    Banished from the complicated world of the far
    future to the barren emptiness of the remote past

The Man in the Maze Robert Silverberg `..    ..` 25p
    Solitary and embittered, hiding from the loathing of
    his fellows, he must be lured out of his refuge to save
    the world

Light a Last Candle Vincent King `..    ..    ..` 25p
    'Vivid stuff, a tale of internecine strife between
    mutated and modified people in the far future.'
    Edmund Cooper, Sunday Times

Farewell, Earth's Bliss D. G. Compton `..    ..` 25p
    Their past was Earth, their present a colony on Mars
    – and their future?

The Time Mercenaries Philip E. High `..    ..    ..` 25p
    They were a thousand years out of date, and the
    planet's only chance to defeat the alien invaders

Donovan's Brain Curt Siodmak `..    ..    ..    ..` 25p
    Doomed by disease, mangled in a plane crash, there
    was no doubt that Donovan was dead. Yet his brain
    lived!

Vornan 19 Robert Silverberg `..    ..    ..    ..` 30p
    He appeared suddenly and mysteriously, claiming
    to be a visitor from the year 2999. But his evidence
    was not totally convincing

Let The Spacemen Beware Poul Anderson `..    ..` 25p
    Why did the gentle people of Gwydonia become like
    savages at Bale-time? And was their strange be-
    haviour connected with the red flower that bloomed
    everywhere on the planet?

Name...

Address ....

Titles required ....

....

....

....

....

....

....

....

The publishers hope that you enjoyed this book and invite you to write for the full list of Tandem titles.

If you find any difficulty in obtaining these books from your usual retailer we shall be pleased to supply the titles of your choice – packing and postage 5p – upon receipt of your remittance.

WRITE NOW TO:
Universal-Tandem Publishing Co. Ltd.,
14 Gloucester Road,
London SW7 4RD